Dedicated to the hope that the few remaining untouched peoples in the world will be able to stay that way... undisturbed, free of all the problems, diseases and stress of modern existence.

All contacted peoples of the Andaman Islands have either disappeared, suffered, or are being irreparably changed by modern contact. The Jarawa of South Andaman Island came out of the forest themselves and that was their choice and cannot be helped. However, those on what we call North Sentinel Island cannot approach us as they are on a reef-fringed island. We would have to approach them.

While T.D Pandit began a wondrous work in the nineties, all contact must now be done by secretive means, after all, the technology now exists to do that. These islanders deserve to remain isolated from western human contact for the own benefit.

They must remain isolated. They are not just guardians of fire by the demands of their existence; they are guardians of a unique existence, and if they are not yet the last - they will certainly be so soon enough by nature of where they live.

They think different to us. They understand life, death and the existence of the world differently to us. I hope this book helps you understand a little more about what life might be like on that tiny 28 square mile island.

The Island

Shelter

Sentinelese

Copyright © 2014 by D.B Daglish
(updated December 2018)

All rights reserved

ISBN 10 - 1502991772
ISBN 13 - 9781502991775

No part of this publication may be reproduced, distributed, or transmitted in any form or by any means, including photocopying, recording, or other electronic or mechanical methods, without the prior written permission of the publisher, except in the case of brief quotations embodied in critical reviews and certain other non-commercial uses permitted by copyright law. For permission requests, write to the publisher at the address below.

D.B Daglish
Manukau, Auckland
New Zealand
Email: dbd@dbdaglish.com
Web: www.dbdaglish.com

Publisher: Naquadah Publishing
Cover: Naquadria Design

All spelling is United States English

The Jangwa* language in the glossary, is copyright to the author

All attempts to locate the owners of photos have been made. If you have ownership of them, I am asking you allow them to stay, so that the people of earth can see the wonder of these wonderful little islanders and how fragile their existence really is in a modern world.

CHAPTERS

1. Isolation
Pre 1867
1867 Homphrey

2. White Spirits of the Sea
1867 MV Nineveh
1880 Portman

3. The Spirit's Walk
1881 Quake and 1.2m tsunami (Port Blair)
1883 Portman
1884 - 1890 quakes

4. They Die like anyone else
Description of a pig hunt
1896 convicts reach shore.

5. The Blending
1895-1910

6. Continuum
Life until 1970

7. Open Defiance
1967-91, T.N. Pandit
1977 – MV Rusley
1981 – MV Primrose

8. Upheaval
1997 Pandit's final visits
2004 – Quake

9. Yaketa
2006 – Fishermen
2011 – Poachers
Concept of time
Fear, quakes & sky demons
2018 - DavidChau

"It's the end of thousands upon thousands of years of history, a whole way of looking at the world is finished, and there's no way of bringing it back."

(Miriam Ross - Spokeswoman for Survival International, in regard to the death of Boa Snr, the last of her race who could still speak the original language of her tribal grouping of Bo, part of the Great Andamanese peoples.)

Introduction

A novel about the Jangwa* people on North Sentinel Island in the Andaman Island chain. Chiö-tá-kwö-kwe is the actual name they themselves call it.

This novel contains information based on what we do know about them, and the incidents recorded since the seventeen hundreds to the present day. However, is it is only a glimpse of what their life might be like, based on similar local tribes. You will see why we should avoid contact with them and let them remain to exist as they are. They do not make fire, but they are guardians of fire - and fire is life.

It is obvious that they should be left alone. Yet even I have a desire to visit and observe how they live. Because that cannot be done with invisibility, any contact will introduce things to their society that would ultimately destroy it. Things such as disease, alcohol and modern ways that would reduce their independence, and make them dependant on outside help, like so many hidden cultures we have stumbled across.

The Ung, in the island to the east, (Jarawa is only the name the Aka-Bea use to describe them), were also untouched once. Nevertheless, they ceased being aggressive and began contact with the Indian settlers who were always encroaching on their land illegally. The Ung's way of life is being altered forever. Already they beg at the side of the road, a road supposedly closed to tourists, yet corrupt Indian officials still allow it. The further from the road they live, the better their way of life. Indian settlers pushed the boundaries that caused conflict with the Ung people. The Onge' to the south are already beyond hope.

Those on Chiö-tá-kwö-kwe deserve better... much better! Being a small isolated island, it is more likely they will remain protected. There is already a 5 km protection zone around the island, yet Indian fishermen are ignored by Coast Guard helicopters as long as they fish the reef edge and do not make any contact with the people. If anyone else got that close, they would be arrested. Yet poaching inside the reef does occur and goes largely unpunished.

Close but non-physical contact was made between 1976-1996 by T.D Pandit, but no direct contact has been made with any Sentinelese people since 1996, (other than two fishermen killed in 2006 who should never have been there in the first place).

If we could be a bird in a tree and see and hear without interference, that would be the most fantastic thing in the world. To understand their language and their simplistic ways and understanding without them knowing we are there, that would be amazing. Until the day we have the technology to do just that, maybe this book may allow a small part of that fantasy to exist in the mind of readers.

This is a small novel, but the purpose is more about education and enlightenment, and hopefully it will result in more people around the world keeping watch to ensure the Indian government continues to protect the vital shores of Chiö-tá-kwö-kwe.

I trust you enjoy reading it as much as I did writing it.

*Jangwa is an assumed name

Isolation

Chiö-á-kwö-kwé could be walked around in a full day of sunlight. Ih had done so many times, yet there was no real purpose in doing so, because if he wanted to visit Juwoi at the beach village on the windward side, he would just use the well-worn tracks. These existed beneath the thick jungle canopy that criss-crossed everywhere between settlements. Near the center, at the highest point on the island, a slight detour was required around one giant tree that had fallen a long time ago, and was now thoroughly eaten out by insects.

On this small island, only five villages existed, and Ih's family group consisted of about 30 individuals at that time. Many generations had lived on his beach for as far back as the stories went, in this case, forty-one of his family's generations. They never counted them as accurately themselves, as their counting was very basic.

Beyond that beginning, they believed they came from somewhere else toward where the sun rises. Well, at least the old Jangwa were in ancient times. The name Jangwa came from the fact they were an isolated people. The Jangil had overrun them and interbreeding occurred after the fight where many died. Ek-Ana, the matriarchal leader managed to quell fighting, drawing the remaining ones together – recounting the stories of the white skinned spirits and the need to repel them. She was wise and her people, though stronger, and having won the battle called themselves a new name, that of the people of Chiö-tá-kwö-kwé. Here, the Jangil really did cease to exist in name, but many of their customs reshaped the culture of that little island.

There was Fo, whom Ih spent a lot of time with whenever he could. He came from the largest village near two bays, separated by a small strip of land, where the land rose gently as it left the ocean. His family could recount their ancestor's back seventy-two names and that took an amazing memory as Ih struggled with just those of his own clan.

The whole island was actually one united group of people, but it still had three distinctions within it. First and most important, the family group living in their own chadda. The second being local groups consisting of about six families including children from other families from elsewhere on the island, as was their custom. They had spread into five locations around the island. Occasionally they would unite in times of trouble or distress at a new village created nearer the island centre. All of those groups made up the Jangwa as a people.

Little happened on this island compared to the world far beyond this isolated existence. Life had been both peaceful and isolated and the island produced all they needed. As far as he knew, this was the world. Yet, he knew of strangers that came over the sea in strange craft that were not of his world. These spirits existed in the sea and ought to be feared.

A story went back twenty four of his elders to Ogi, where the earliest known contact of strange looking people who did not have dark skin like themselves, the Jangil, Ung or Onge.

Yet no one had seen any other living individual since Gafo led the fight against those from across the sea some eight generation's earlier. They were the Onge, and not as fierce as the Ung, according to the stories. Only one survivor of that fracas, Ibo, pleading to live, after seeing those around him killed. They allowed him to stay with them.

The Onge, or Eng-nga as they called themselves, had tried a clever ruse. Many warriors lay down in their large craft, ready to leap up and appear at the last moment as Gafo and his warriors stood in the shallows. Gafo had been motionless, waiting to see if the contact was friendly or not. He knew from earlier stories, not to trust any contact. It seemed, to the visitors, that those on the island were unarmed. But they were caught by surprise when as they leaped from their position, weapons in hand, and entered the water yelling and expecting an easy victory, Gafo called out in a loud voice. As one man, the warriors stooped down into the water and produced weapons that they had been standing on, unseen in the sand of the shallows.

A barrage of arrows from the tree line, and the more accurate flurry from the beach repelled the invaders and two fell, fatally pierced with arrows longer than a man's arm. One was surrounded by other warriors and he fell to his knees. The rest fled to their dugout's and quickly retreated out into the lagoon. More arrows met their mark as the En-iregale paddled out toward the entrance in the reef and out of sight.

"Perfect people they are not," mocked Sik, in reference to the name the Onge used for themselves.

Then he turned to the one who knelt in the sand surrounded by Jangwa youth who pointed arrows at the prisoner.

Fo called them to separate so those in the retreating canoes could see clearly, and he hit the Onge on the head with his hand, telling him to stay down on his knees. Many Jangwa rushed to bring their crude dugout canoes out of the tree line to pursue, but were called back. They could not follow as their dange' were not built for ocean travel. There was no need to chase anyway, as he assumed they would not return, and he did not want to risk any craft or any man in a futile attempt to kill more. The breakers at any ocean reef are dangerous and it surprised Fo the invaders had been able to arrive, let alone leave so easily. Fo did not consider the tide. It was extremely high that day.

His attention now returned to the lone Eng-nga still cowering in the sand, certain his life would end. Gofo raised his club but the invader cried out and they realized they could understand part of what he said and the intent of his words.

"No!" Fo ordered, and Gofo lowered the club to his side.

"You want to live?" Fo asked of the man cowering in the sand. A puzzled look came upon his face and he put his hands on the back of his head in submission.

"Live," he said in a garbled version of their word.

The tip of Fo's bow touched under his chin and Ibo raised his head in obedience. He was aware of the danger...of death occurring at any moment - even being eaten. He did not know that Jangwa do not eat humans as they had been told. In fact, no tribes in those islands did, but he would not find out until his grasp of the language improved.

These islands had a reputation in the outside world of cannibalism. This was because the Jangwa burned bodies in fire to purge the evil spirits within the bodies. Anyone watching this would make certain assumptions.

"We should kill him!" called Sik loudly as he raised his bow, already fitted with an arrow and aimed directly at Ibo's chest. A bow tip suddenly pushed on top of the arrow, forcing his aim to the sand. He submitted quickly. For Asi had put taken hold of a bow and forced his arrow downward.

"No Sik, we do not need to kill him," and she walked closer, placing a hand on Ibo's head.

"I claim him as a slave," she said. Her husband shot a cool glance at her.

Asi was a strong woman. She had the ear of most on the island and being Fo's wife, she commanded an unspoken respect and power within the communities of Chiö-tá-kwö-kwé.

"He is En-iregale, not Ung, so not as hostile...besides..." she said. "Did they attack first? All I saw were more of them standing up than we first could see."

In this way, Asi saved Ibo's life, and he remained bound to a tree in the village for the first few days as they fed him hand to mouth. As days went by, he was free to walk but with bound hands. Eventually he was untied and encouraged to take part in daily life; but closely watched until the time came to test him.

Ibo was treated kindly, and Asi had not really intended to keep him as a slave. He had even been allowed to get close to weapons, with unseen armed men hiding at a distance ready with arrow fitted to their bows. He knew they were there and ignored them, which saved his life. He suspected a trap and besides, he did not intend to kill anyone.

The real test was would he try to flee? A small two man dange' remained at the water's edge as others walked back to the village with a catch of fish. Ibo was ordered to pull it into the tree line by himself. Once again warriors were stationed ready to fire should he attempt to flee but to their astonishment he stood there for a long time looking at the reef, strangely quiet for the season, then seeing him grab a paddle they fitted arrows to their bows. Tossing the paddle into the dange', Ibo dragged the craft up into the tree line and followed the track back to the village on his own.

There was never any intent to escape. However, if he were to let them know of his awareness of the warriors that watched him, they may not trust him further, and he desperately needed that trust - for he wanted to stay anyway.

The Onge are a sterile people. Few children were ever born, and his own wife at home had never produced a single child. He noticed the women of the Jangwa were slightly taller. They lacked the big buttocks but they had pleasant facial features. What is more, one of the older girls showed an interest in him. It was she who had managed a discrete meeting alone up on the slopes of Oon where the split rocks produced a path and a hollow, all hidden under the canopy of trees. From the tops of the trees on Oon, one could see the entire island. Rubbing noses had begun what they could not stop. Asi was aware of this of course, and she kept it quietly to herself.

When Ibo finally died, his family buried him in among the roots of one of the trees. Though not at the normal sacred place around the rocks, it was within sight of them. Far enough away to suggest he was not one of them and yet close enough to show connection. This satisfied Asi, who by then was a very old woman. Ibo's bones were the ones discovered in the late eighteen hundreds by a British search party.

Matah was in his forties. He remembered clearly the day long ago when the ground shook, and he rushed his family to higher ground, making sure they stayed there until the roar of waves came later in the day. Once they returned to the beach they could see that little remained untouched and it took some time to recover what the waves had scattered. Shelters were easily rebuilt, but weapons and talisman were valuable, and these had been the only items carried with them when they fled. Just a few bows hidden in the sands were lost. However, much debris was scattered and a plentiful supply of the large hard seed, Nariele with its soft white center, had washed up everywhere. None could remember such a shaking happening in their lifetime but stories had been told of it occurring before.

Yet here again, the ground had shaken violently, trees swayed wildly and many fell, their leaves floated down like rain and birds filled the air. Matah found it hard to stand up; the quake was so violent. As moving the ground lessened, he called for everyone to move to higher ground, making sure all items able to be carried went with them. Even the dange' were dragged further up the slope. When all was as safe as he could make it, he took off through the forest tracks to Ki on the other side to see how they fared.

Thankfully, just a few large waves reached across the reef through the day, and only a few trees were uprooted unlike what he remembered as a child. On the sand of the beach something strange lay. It was like a large coconut with flat ends. It was heavy so Matah called for help to roll it up the sand to the shelter of the tree line.

They brought fire back from their safety point and more fires were lit as darkness fell. Torches are always prepared and ready for transporting fire to other locations should the need arise. Fire was something the Jangwa both cherished and protected. If the fires went out, it would only become available again when fire from the sky fell during storms. A few Jangil brought this practice of keeping torches burning. They persuaded Koj to allow them to live there to avoid the white man and the brown ones who invaded their island. This island, its trees and environment was almost the same as where they had lived. Their shelters, weapons and language had similarities also.

A shrill call went up along the beach from where some were still fishing. Late morning arrived and this was time to come in and take advantage of the shade of the forest for the hottest part of the day. As their eyes followed the direction Togi pointed, they could see something strange appearing around the edge of the island from the direction of the horizon.

The call spread quickly through the forest until a dozen or so men assembled on the beach as something large neared their island outside the confines of the reef. It floated like a dugout log, yet much larger. Its white wings seemed to flap as if it were a sea eagle trying to gain flight after taking a large fish from the sea.

They had been seen before, but at a great distance. This one however, was close enough that one could paddle to it just beyond the reef.

Ukla placed his hand over his brow seeking to shade the suns reflection on the water. He became afraid, as it appeared as if men moved on it, mostly white like the spirits of the sea they had been taught about, but also three shorter black figures.

He assumed these were dead Ung, and maybe one of them was Kaj who had drowned and whose body was never found. Without a proper burial, such a person might remain a hostile spirit. They did not wish to have contact with these white spirits, as death was the only result, so they stood, transfixed, to see what would occur - ready to flee, but mesmerized at the wonder of the sight before them.

The small black figures disappeared from view and the white spirits moved about all over the thing on which they floated. There were many waves on the reef on this side of the island. Ukla was aware that with the size of them, not much would be crossing into the lagoon, but he feared they still might try. What horrors could come if the spirits of the sea were to make land in such numbers?

His fear disappeared when, within a short time, the winged craft moved away from the reef edge and out of sight toward the direction of the place where legend said fire came from the sea.

White Spirits of the Sea

Two seasons passed and a violent storm had already raged for three days. Its strength was enough for everyone to leave the beach shelters and venture inland to the large communal huts deep in the forest. Once the violent winds subsided, they trekked back to the sea to find a child running back with fear written all over his face.

"Etobabu," he cried, as many people were on the beach. "Ani-Onu," he said, rubbing his hands over his face. A frightened look came over their faces also. "Sea spirits...? On the beach?"

Carefully they approached to find a large number of people assembled. In fact, it appeared there might be more of them than all the Jangwa that existed on the island. The skin on their faces was white and yet they had a covering over their entire bodies with just the faces exposed. A large thing with torn wings perched on their reef much like what passed in the distance from time to time. It looked as though they had begun eating something.

Ukla thought that maybe they were spirits. Stories suggested they can be killed, but here many existed, far too many to fight successfully, yet fight they did. Carefully spreading out the warriors along and around those on the beach, they let fly a volley of arrows.

"Go away," they screamed at them amid the shouts of the large volume of people. Four arrows finally found their mark. They could not see any blood from the wounds and assumed the spirits absorbed the arrows; such was the confusion of the moment. However, they only had a limited number of arrows and they soon they ran out.

In response to the attack, nearly eighty of the spirits retaliated with much yelling, throwing a barrage of stones at Ukla and his people. Several loud noises split the air and Tal fell with a severe wound to his shoulder yet no one noticed anything hitting him. Ike also fell with a severe gash to the head from a thrown rock, others were pelted severely and a hand-to-hand fight occurred. Boke stabbed one of the males but was quickly beaten back by several spirits with sticks picked up from the beach.

The sound of the fear and screaming the women joined with the wild shrill yells of his own people, made for quite a scene. Eventually they retreated into the jungle, close enough to see, yet far enough back not to be in any danger. With all arrows dispatched, the Jangwa had none left as the strangers had picked up what had fallen around them. The smaller craft with a few men was on its way back to the ocean, passing the large one stuck firmly on the reef leaving the rest behind on the beach. By evening fires roared and as the strangers were armed with sticks, rocks and some other things of unfamiliar form. All the Jangwa retired into the forest except a few who stayed to watch. If any of the invaders ventured into the forest alone, they would not return.

Tal's shoulder wound was very bad and he would never regain full use of it again.

For three days they kept a careful eye on them until the strangers left in groups by means of a large wide dange'. They could be seen climbing into a large floating craft with the white wings. Once all had left, they searched for their arrows but few were found. The Jangwa stripped much wood and iron from the wreck. Nothing happened to them upon entering the spirits craft, and they decided that these people were not spirits after all, and the fact they finally saw some bleed after the attack. However, all agreed they should still be avoided, at all costs.

Kogio stayed and watched as the strangers left. The wind was blowing up the island and he saw the wings stop moving, change then stay put as the craft followed the wind. He picked up a palm leaf in his hand and felt the pull of the wind against the leaves and as he let it go, it travelled an arm's length before hitting the sand. He put a leaf in a piece of driftwood and noticed how the wind played with it. The Jangwa knew much about the wind - they could even smell changes upon it. Yet the significance of what he witnessed was lost to him, but he did laugh at his creation as it blew out into the lagoon.

The following day as he finished fishing, he pushed a large dead leaf into a small piece of wood and waded out up to his thighs.

"What are you doing?" Pi asked.

"Look," he said as he let it drift, watching the wind carry it across the lagoon, and then collecting his catch from the beach they returned to the camp. Forgetting his discovery that day, they lost what was so nearly an adaptation based on an observation of another race.

Once again, the time of year for collecting le was upon them. On this side of the island, Boke was the most observant, and he saw a new hive in an easy position. Snapping a few branches to point out he had seen it first, he returned to the camp.

"Le, I have found le," he said, and at that, a cry of joy went up. Le was their favorite food. Sweet and runny, the white sticky stuff that held it together was used on weapons and bows to stop the wood from splitting. For some reason, bees had been scarce for a time and had only seemed to grow in number again since the last two rainy seasons.

They followed him back to the location, all willing to help because le was especially sought after, and all helped retrieve it. Although all shared in it, the finder always had the rights to the first taste. If only a small find, they would eat it in the forest. However, if the find were large enough, it would be taken back to the camps, and kept in baskets covered in leaves to keep other insects out.

Boke chewed the leaves of a plant they called tonjoghe jah. Three types of plant they could use with similar result, but this was the first he located in his search and always the most potent. He started smearing the chewed substance over his body and others helped smear it over what he could not reach.

Stuffing his mouth with more leaves, he climbed up the tree toward the hive high in the tree.

The scent of the leaves on his body kept the insects at bay although one found an unprotected spot on his leg. This was the first time he had ever been stung, for this plant mixture had an effect of calming numbing the bees; keeping them docile for a long time.

The nest hung low beneath the branch and the noise of the many bees could be heard by those far below on the forest floor. Carefully Boke moved out, straddling the branch until within touching distance. At this height, to fall now would be certain death. The leaves he chewed were now just a paste in his mouth. Gently he leaned forward and breathed upon the nest. The affect was immediate as the bees dropped to the ground and those clinging to the nest ceased to move. They were not dead but immobilized. This practice had been taught for generations, yet none knew why it worked. However, the why was not as important as result.

Carefully he cut the hive below the branch leaving a little for the bees to rebuild from. Being of good size, this hive hung rather low and he had to stretch to cut with one hand while holding onto the branch with the other. Most nests were narrow, and about the length of his arm. Pulling it up and onto the branch where he sat, cutting off lengths small enough to fit into the wooden Uhu he carried. This container was fashioned for the express purpose of holding le. It had been with his people for as long as any could remember. Of course, they did not understand the wax was what preserved the wood for so many generations.

Gently he lowered the Uhu down on its rope until those below could grab it, then he let go of the rope and it fell to the forest floor. Replacing the knife in his belt, he began to work his way back, quickly clambering down as nimble as a squirrel to those gathered below on the forest floor. The honeycomb pieces were held up as Boke breathed on them once again and then spat the mixture out. The remaining bees fell to the ground and the group retired to the buttress roots of a large tree nearby to consume the honey, one crushing a scorpion with a stone as it scuttled by. Le was always a welcome addition to their seasonal and revolving pattern of food that had existed for as long as time began.

Four full moons had come and gone. Most of the camps shifted from the marsh area where the sun sets, to the other end of the island. The white spirits landed once more, trekking through the forest but failing to reach the main village near the opposite end of the island. Here, the village sat on a raised area that sloped steeply down to the water's edge. There a tree grew, and Picha-Enriya would climb to where he could see the coast and reef without going down to the beach. Here they spent a lot of time during the rainier season, where run off moved away from the village. It was drier and with a slight breeze due to level of elevation and the spacing of the trees, therefore cooler than the still, damp air of the forest.

Naili saw the white spirits as she hunted for tubers. They were walking along one of the lesser used tracks for this time of year. Staying well hidden in the undergrowth and behind the large trees and buttress roots, she followed them as they headed back up to the summer camp area, and watched the strangers leave. They were following the common tracks through the jungle and appeared to have come up from the beach area where one could see the lands of the Ya-enga-nga and the Ung. This fact was instrumental in them failing to find the village of eighteen huts, for the permanent village was not accessed by a direct route through the middle. This was just as well as these strangers; they now called Ya-enga-Paluga-wa, may have found it. There was a direct route to the beach below and one toward the open ocean but it was new village that had been constructed since coming off the beaches. There were few permanent tracks to it.

The following day was sunnier with a gentler breeze. It was reported that the Ya-enga-Paluga-wa had returned and this time they were coming and going from the floating thing they arrived in. During the day, some camped near the beach close to the swamp area. This was not a good place during the rainy season and Ukla commented that the white spirits did not seem very bright.

"They may be immune to the insects," suggested another, "they are spirits!"

Ukla agreed, but doubted their ferociousness. They were supposed to eat human flesh, but better to try to kill one than be eaten by one. Yet he was thinking they had been unable to find the village a few days before. Surely, spirits could see all around them, yet the Jangwa had remained hidden from their sight or knowledge. This was not what was expected of all-powerful spirits.

Boke's village was on the sheltered side of the island. He had to flee once, as they heard the strangers come through the jungle and on return found weapons missing, among them many arrows with various barbed bone tips. In exchange, some very strange things were left in their place. One was a hard substance that he could see through. It had no purpose so he threw it to the edge of the camp. Yet the next morning they came again as the men had left camp to hunt. Upon return, they discovered the Ya-enga-Paluga-wa had taken a woman and four children.

Boke was incensed and frightened, as he believed they were taken away to be eaten. For four days, he mourned and discussion was held between those of all three villages as to what to do. He reported that the spirits lit a fire on the small island at the top of the island and feared his family had been cooked and eaten.

As they sat down around their own fire, warming themselves for the beginning of the day, Naili suddenly appeared with the children with a strange and disturbing tale to tell. Her arrival caused several to be frightened thinking Naili and the children were actually spirits returning, but she assured them it was her, alive and unharmed. She did not know, but had met M.V Portman the British Officer in charge of the Andamanese. This was her story that everyone on the island heard the following day.

"We were surprised and seized by these spirits, bound and taken back to our summer camps. They took us to a strange dange' and taken over the reef to a very large one with the wings attached. We were untied and we had to climb up vines to get into it. They are not fierce, but we could not understand them at all. They smiled a lot at us. Handed us things and took our hand in one of theirs for some reason. They fed us but I spat it out at first. We were watered and covered in something strange. The things we could see amazed us, the children, particularly Kanoi and Kanjo, were interested in everything. They killed a bird without an arrow. They used a stick that made a loud noise and the bird they pointed it at fell to the sea where they fetched it. The thing we were on they called a 'Sep'. It was solid, made of trees and we could go under the water without getting wet. I was scared with that but it held water out like our dugouts, but it is deeper, much deeper at least two lengths wide and two lengths deep," she said.

Looks of wonder filled the faces of those listening. With such intense interest she continued.

"Their faces are white but everything else is covered. We saw one with his upper body uncovered. They have hair all over, not just the faces. They showed us places to sleep on something soft like skins, but we went back up to sleep up in the open air. There were no insects at night out on the sea. The movement kept us awake. They sang to us and made me sing to them the second day. But I became lonely and scared the third day and kept pointing to the beach. Today they brought us back and I saw a number go to Apilai'oh and camp there. Nine of them there was. We are not harmed, but I still fear them…yet…" and she ended her story while much discussion followed deep into the night.

A few days later Fo was with his wife Asi and a new baby. He was old by all standards in this environment and as far as anyone could remember, Asi was the oldest to have received a child. They were returning to the main village when they happened to be surprised by a party of spirits. Up close, they looked just as Naili had described them, but there also some brown ones among them. They fanned themselves out across the path and into the forest around about. Fo quickly put an arrow to his bowstring and aimed at the one in the centre who approached him.

"Leave, leave," he yelled, as he threatened the tall one in the centre. He pulled the string back, aimed at the tall ones head, and was about to fire when an attack came from behind. Big burley arms encircled him preventing him from discharging his arrow. Quickly the one that held his arms wrestled him to the ground. Asi shrilled loudly until she too was set upon and a hand put over her mouth. Others grabbed the four children, they were taken away toward the beach to the same place Naili, and her children had been taken. He could recognize it from her description but nothing could prepare him for the reality.

The 'sep' Naili had described, took them across the sea. Fo was restrained and prevented from jumping overboard until the island was far enough behind for the risk of a jumping to have gone. He realized the direction of travel was toward the land of the Onge' and the Jangil and maybe even the Ung, who he remembered were very fierce. They passed between the islands of the Jangil and where the Aka-Bea lived. As a child, he had been told of this place and he feared them, but did not know why.

As they came into a large bay he was astounded to see, not forest down to the water's edge, but cleared areas and strange structures everywhere and many more 'sep's' and other strange things. On the voyage, an Aka'Bea, a native of the larger island, closely watched him. He could not understand anything he said although a few words were familiar to some degree. "Home" and "friendly" were the only two words he thought he could understand. Fo and his family were kept in a strange hut with holes in the walls where one could look out. A flat wooden plank that swung two ways was the only way in or out. He inspected the latch. It was made of the same material they found sometimes on the beach and the same material found on the 'sep'.

Many strange and fearsome people came to look at them and touch them. He had seen many white faces but never the brown ones. It seemed the most important ones were those with the white faces. They were the ones in charge.

Fo had no concept of hierarchy, rulers or power of individuals. No ruler existed on Chiö-tá-kwö-kwé, and the only ones who held more sway in decisions than others were those who could see the spirits and talk to them. However, in this place, some held more reverence than others did. The brighter the colors of their coverings the more important Fo surmised.

Over three days, they had all sorts of visitors, were forced to bathe with the insistence of some who took them and held them while washed and covered in strange garb. They felt heavy and uncomfortable, but warmer at night. The children were left naked although 'naked' was not a concept any Andamanese ever considered. They were only allowed out of the structure with the brown ones following closely behind.

A few days later Fo and Asi became sick. They were coughing and sneezing, things which they had never encountered before and they became frightened, fearing death. Fo spoke to his children not be scared as all life returned, yet if he wasn't buried properly he might not return as he wished he could. Within two days, Fo and Asi were both dead.

The four children were soon herded to the same thing that brought them to this place, after watching their parents buried in a hole and covered over. They were unceremoniously dumped off at the same beach they had left from, after being captured. With them were many strange things some of which they had seen at the whiter spirits large village. Quickly they ran back to their village frightened but happy they were home at last. Around the fire, they reported all they had seen and even where the whites hung three browns by the neck off a strange tree. The browns could die and they had seen one white spirit bleeding freely from his head and body and being helped by two others as he passed them.

It was certain they could be hit with arrows as the first foray sometime before had proved but no one had seen any sign of injury as a result. To have seen one bleeding profusely interested Ukla, and the anger festered because his parents were dead, killed by those that took them and could not be buried according to their customary ways.

Enraged, he knew he could not take revenge on these 'spirits' yet…if a 'spirit' could bleed? Someone needed to test if one could die, to see if they were spirits from the sea, or man of a different kind, which he now suspected they might be.

They were careful to avoid the visitors from the sea every day after that, if they were known to be here. Small camps on five locations, each with three people, were set up so they would not be surprised again. Thereafter, the villages were on alert, and the young among them stationed along the tracks to keep watch during the day. In this way, they could warn of anyone approaching, in case those at the beach lookouts were quickly overrun.

The Spirits Walk

After the white spirits of the sea came, a full set of seasons passed when the ground shook violently. Lololoköbey was occurring and it proved the ancestral spirits were angry. Angry with the white people or angry that the Jangwa had not defended their land? They could not agree on which. Immediately they gathered on the shores with their baskets, bows and arrows and took apart all the accumulated pig and turtle skulls, and threw them into the sea. Finally, they hurled a few stones at the sea and then rapidly left the coast, moving inland and up the slopes for protection. The purpose of the skull throwing was to trick the spirits into thinking the community had drowned when the water passed over, both them and the stones they threw.

Lololoköbey was a natural event in the order of things. As with previous generations, they accepted what happened, followed the ritual and went inland like all their ancestors had done many times before them. They knew instinctively that when the sea receded at a rapid rate, it would eventually return with great power and even greater speed. The good spirits want to provide order to the sea and forest on which the Jangwa depend. The bad spirits sometimes try to cause death to the humans when they feel the need to produce more members of their kind. They shake the trees that support the sea and hurl boulders that cause large waves and when the Jangwa flee, they hope that at least one might suffer an unplanned death.

If they claimed a body before the Jangwa could recover it, the individual becomes a malevolent spirit. This is why in battle, all Jangwa carry their wounded and leave none behind. Killing humans produces dead, and the lololoköbey allowed the dead to pass over to the otherworld as spirits. If buried properly, they would be good spirits.

Nevertheless, this shaking had occurred after Fo and Asi were buried in a hole by the whites, not on home soil and definitely not according to custom. After all, they believed that order must emerge from disorder to provide permanence of their culture and beliefs.

With this event, the waves appeared small compared with stories told of events in the ancestor's days. Temporary shelters on the shoreline washed away, but these were easily replaced. They lost a few items, but no weapons or useful items, and no loss of life occurred. During lololoköbey, the spirits were asked for help and they sought that another will be born to them and in fact, five moon cycles later, little Gabeke was born. Four cycles later Gafo was born, a boy bigger than most babies, longer and certainly more alert.

Then yet another birth occurred some moon cycles afterward. The Jangwa did not have a high birthrate and they took this new birth as a blessing. On the night of Enmie's birth, loud sounds came from the sky and startled them. Many were afraid, for no story ever told around the fires involved this type of occurrence. Morning came and even larger sounds occurred unlike anything anyone remembered and all became extremely frightened. The sea did not recede as it would before rushing into the trees, as it would after a ground shaking. Birds left the trees and flew around in greater numbers never seen before. For some reason the sky spirits were angry. Adults knew the stories. They rushed their families off the beach and up the slopes into the jungles, just high enough to be safe should the waves come.

Later, in the darkness, they heard wave surges pounding the reef at low tide. They could hear little crashing through the trees unlike other times when large waves washed away coastal structures and camps. All permanent villages remained inland and on higher slopes as time long-ago had taught them to do.

A strange acrid smell followed the wind from the direction where the sun would rise. This morning was darker than normal and the day was even darker as the sky turned red and then brown and sometimes almost black. Most cowered in their huts, eyes burning slightly as a few went to the coast to see what had occurred. Very little damage was apparent on the beaches. The sea had risen a little, and all camps visited seemed largely intact, but one. All dange' were eventually found, including one washed inland near the low-lying swampy area.

The following day the Ya-enga-Paluga-wa once again set foot on Chiö-tá-kwö-kwé. Word passed quickly through the forest, and all fled to safe areas away from the villages. For the first time, the strangers appeared around the large central village. It was deserted, or so they thought. From the shadows, and behind the tree root buttresses, several eyes watched every move, armed and ready should the need arise. If the Ya-enga-Paluga-wa had been aware of the number of arrows aimed at them, they might have been worried. Yet no signal was given, for the whites took nothing, but left a few items behind. In fact, they left items in every shelter on the island that they could find, and then departed.

Nervousness swept through the Jangwa encampments as they were aware the balance had been disturbed in the spirit world. It was confirmed that the spirits were indeed angry when almost one set of seasons later, the earth shook violently once more. This time there was no falling trees and no large waves from the spirits. Three new children were born after the last shaking and now it seemed the spirits wanted more people back for their numbers to swell, but none were taken, and none had fallen ill. The Jangwa were confused regarding all these events.

Ukla was still concerned, but Kogio, as always, was a thinker. "Things are on our side," he insisted. "White spirits come, yet none of us have died, none have been killed, we have new children, Kanjo killed his first Kue on his own and avoided the teeth. I do not think they are angry enough. Let us wait and see, but be ready. Store weapons in various places so we are never unprepared and always have a store of arrows should we use all we carry up in one fight."

Kanjo had recently killed his first kue and it was of excellent size. He did not know Fo, the second in recent memory to have that name, had been herding it all day and Kanjo was directed to it, once it was already tired. Yet no one said anything to any young hunter - they usually found out later when other children were put through the rite of passage to kill a boar, and they smiled knowingly that they too were deceived.

Humor was constant on the island and tricks were often played upon each other and not just by children. Fo, one of their oldest, was particularly good at playing tricks and many were sad that he died elsewhere, as he had. Sometimes it seemed that some tricks occurred that no one ever owned up to, and Ukla he wondered if Fo had become a mischievous spirit?

Nevertheless, the weapon's idea was one they knew, but had forgotten to practice. Years of isolation had allowed this practice to fall away. Ukla then discussed this with all the villagers, and stores of arrows were thereafter kept in hollow tree trunks around the island and near the coast. They were checked, swapped or replaced as needed over the years.

Now two sets of seasons had come and gone since the sounds in the sky and the sea surges. During that time two visits of the whites had occurred. The Jangwa all fled and hid as they did in earlier events. Once again, strange items were left including pieces of Che, like they found washed up on the reef from time to time. From this, they fashioned arrowheads and spear tips. The Che was hard to shape but could be sharpened with stone and protected with the honey wax they called le-mal.

However, this visit was different. From their hiding places, they could see some with them that looked as they themselves were. Short, black... Ung maybe?

"En-iregale? They look like Ibo did. Remember his hair he kept different?" said Fuh.

Indeed Portman had brought Onge from the island to the south with him to try to communicate with those on the island. They had managed to creep through the jungle quietly until they came to a place where they could see some of the inhabitants of Chiö-tá-kwö-kwé. Bows were drawn but none fired any arrows. As they spoke in their shrill chatter, the Onge called out to them.

Silence fell quickly among them. Most of it made no sense but one word sounded familiar… "bei-cam-be!"

"Be-Cha-bu?" Boke asked. "Are they are warning us or helping us?"

Ukla called back, but the only response was one they could not understand.

"It may not mean what we think it does. They are not threatening to kill us. Does anyone see weapons?"

No response came from any of them.

"Let us approach then. Load an arrow", he said as they advanced toward who they believed were Eng-nga. A warning arrow whistled through the air and the strangers turned and left, seemingly not afraid for they did not run.

"I do not believe we have anything to fear from them," Ukla suggested.

"Why are they with the white spirits? Are they dead?"

"No", said Kogio, who had moved to where they had been. "Do spirits leave footprints?"

Indeed, on a damp patch of ground they could see small footprints showing five toe imprints. They knew the whites did not leave human footprints as they had no toes, so they were still regarded as spirits.

The Onge reported to Portman "ekw-ako-belat-elebeg," meaning 'they came running at them.' Portman became frustrated with the lack of meaningful contact, even when using Onge.

Back at the village, tales of a heroic fight and defeat of a warring tribe delivered by the white spirits had begun. The story was gradually added to, so by the next morning it was firmly set in the minds of all that heard it. This story was told often, and remembered by Ih long into his life.

Kanjo had speared three small kalo, the last one still thrashing about in the base of dange'. Now twenty years old he had taken young Kanji out fishing with him. It was Kanjo who was confronted by yet another visit of whites. Quickly they poled the dugout to shore, pulled it into the bushes and fled into the interior, warning those in the new village sites as they ran. Once confirmed that the strangers had left, a discussion occurred regarding one they kept seeing repeatedly.

The face of this visitor was not fully covered in hair, as the spirits of the sea were supposed to have. For under his nose a strange type of hair grew. This individual was usually surrounded by other whites, and a few browns every time whites came to the island. They had noticed the last few times that nothing was missing from their chadda's, unlike many years before when items always seem to be taken.

For some time nothing occurred, and a period of inner calm came to the inhabitants of Chiö-tá-kwö-kwe. The population even grew at little once again. It was the time between the two rainy seasons and most of the inhabitants encamped at the top of the island near the tidal marsh area. Just out from the beach a small island existed, the same little islet the tall white one had stayed at many years before.

Yet again, the white wings of the 'sep' were spotted before any of those upon it could see them. All dange' but one had been dragged ashore and everyone in potential view of the 'sep', hid at the edge of the low forest in the shadows. They learned not to build shelters in full view of the sea now and most were now concealed, well within the forest shadows.

They watched cautiously as the large vessel moved away out of sight and so slowly, the Jangwa came back to the reef. A dugout with Kanoi and two others were near the outer edge of the reef, just past the small peninsula connected to the mainland by low-lying land. It was rare to go outside the protection of the reef, but with certain bait, they could lure the large fish to the surface and shoot them with the arrows designed for this purpose. A calm sea was needed to enable them to go beyond the safety of the lagoons, and today was such a day. Yet, suddenly the 'sep' returned. Jangwa had no paddles, only poles, but out here, their wide bows were able to propel them along slowly. Flight was going to be difficult, so they stopped and watched to see what would happen. Bows were gripped tightly and arrows, the ones Konoi had suggested they make for warning, were readied. These longer ones would travel further, but did not have any tips of the hard substance; therefore, all they would waste would be the shafts, which were quickly made from the branches of the taboi-da. These branches were long, straight, and hardened nicely when exposed to fire for a short time.

Konoi could clearly see a number of people as the vessel came within five or six lengths of the dugout away. They were afraid as they became vulnerable in the open sea. White spirits were seen talking and pointing and smaller darker ones that appeared as well. Eng-nga he assumed, as he could not understand them. They looked as the story of previous battles had described, with their testicles covered or bound. The Jangwa however, wore only a bark waist protector and nothing else.

The warning arrows were now fitted to their bows and loosely pointed at those in the vessel. He heard shouting of the white ones and several pointed strange sticks at them. Konoi recognized what they were from his time aboard years before. More frantic calls came from the En-iregale trying to warn the Jangwa, but it just added to the confusion as they yelled back for them not to come near them. Those aboard could see the fear in the natives eyes and then they heard words they did understand as one appeared and spoke to them directly. Not all words they could understand, but enough to know there was one aboard who knew their language. They feared he was a rogue spirit of one of their dead, but the face was not one they recognized, and he was not fully understandable. Whatever he did say, the intent became clear enough. Arrows were dropped, and their bows were now used as paddles as they frantically they made their way back inside the reef. Here, poles were used to propel them back toward the beach as fast as possible.

Suddenly some items hit the sea round them, one hitting Foh-te-enge on the back of the head. Konoi was about to fit an arrow to his bow when he realized they were coconuts, and suggested they keep moving as they were not weapons of attack. When they turned to look back, the visitors had already begun to move away out into the deep ocean beyond where any living Jangwa had ever been. They stopped and checked Foh-te-enge's head. He had a large and growing bump and some blood flowed down his neck, but he was not badly hurt, at least not physically. However, his emotional state was not one of calm, considering the 'spirits' had thrown things at him.

Three coconuts lay in the bottom of the dange' including the one that had hit the boys head. Behind them, they could see more floating in the sea and they returned to collect them, all the while discussing the encounter.

By the time two more dange' reached them, and as typical with all natives of these lands, the story was already deemed to be somewhat more dramatic. They were still a distance from the shore where many had gathered and much discussion ensued as they were helped to the beach.

That evening, once Ukla had returned from a gathering le, he heard the story as it was now told, including the words Konoi, Foh-te-enge and Bowa-ya had heard from the one Eng-nga.

"You are sure?" Ukla asked.

"I heard the words myself. He said if we raised our arrows, we would die. I understood him, yet he was not one of us...unless...he was... spirit...?" Kanoi paused as he thought for a while.

"The sticks they pointed I have seen before. They make a frightening noise and things they point at fall dead. I have seen it. The Eng-nga confirmed what I knew; he was trying to save us I think."

"Who was he?" Kogio asked. "A spirit ancestor or a living person... Dauwacho maybe?"

Now Kanoi remembered. "He told me his name!" he declared and all went silent. Spirits did not retain their names, and they waited for him to continue.

"He said Bo. Who is Bo?"

"But Bo is dead. He went missing a long time ago." Naili declared. She knew Bo as a child because Bo was her elder sister's son.

"His body was ever found. Maybe Dauwacho took him with him. If he made the islands of the En-iregale, they may have taken Bo as a slave even if they killed Dauwacho. He would be the right age by now to fit what Kanoi says he was." Kogio offered.

"So..." he said looking again at Kogio, "Your knowledge, and Bo, may have saved some lives today. Now we know they have weapons greater than ours. We need to be careful. A better understanding began to emerge as best it could among a people devoid of knowledge of anything outside forest life.

Kogio was the first and only Jangwa to have abilities beyond those around him. Little toy dugouts with large leaves were now used on the water's edge as the children wondered at the wind carrying their toys out to sea beyond their sight. This practice eventually died out for an unknown reason.

They die like anyone else

Three small natural springs existed on the island. The main source was in the limestone on a flat ridge below the highest point of the island. The others were at either end, one no more than a muddy hole the pigs mainly used. Fo took no more than a glance at the former as he walked by. He has no idea of how fragile life would become if these two water sources dried up. Of course, they also collected water when it rained, but the dry months required use of the spring water.

At the top of trees, the wind blew steady and strong, but on the forest floor very little moved - so dense was the canopy above them. Still, it was always the way to ensure you approached your quarry from the opposite direction from where the wind came from and Fo was doing just that. It was rare for any woman to come on a kue hunt. It was traditionally a male only event, as boar are very dangerous. Yet, one woman in their history had been a prolific hunter. The story of Timu-le, was often told around the village fires at night.

Seven men slowly approached, fanning out with bows drawn as best they could among the thick underbrush. Just ahead, lay the watering area the pigs most often used.

They would never attack at the watering hole, but they did use the pig's one real sense... smell. An attack from downwind might bring you very close to the creature with poor sight and hearing. The kue caught the scent of Kanjo, coming from the opposite direction exactly as had been planned.

On three of the commonly used paths created by the pigs, men quietly waited. Grunting sounds filled the forest and leading the flight, one of the younger boars appeared just as Ukla stepped into the path. Seeing the human, the boar turned sharply to the left as an arrow pierced its side. The boar squealed loudly, and those in wait succeeded in having two more out of eight arrows reaching their target. Bursting into the thick underbrush with incredible velocity, the wounded animal proceeded to put as much distance between those that it feared and itself, but it found the going tougher than usual.

On isolated Chiö-tá-kwö-kwé, the Jangwa had the same type of hunting techniques as the islands of the Onge' or Ung. They used a special arrow with a detachable head for hunting pigs. Unlike standard fishing arrows of bamboo tipped with hardwood, these arrows were meticulously shaped. Honed from a single branch of hardwood until straight to the eye, and then stuck in the ground to be dried and hardened by a slow burning fire. When hitting target such as a boar, the detachable head would hold and the shaft would come away. This would flail about in the underbrush catching on various plants and eventually slowing down the fleeing animal. In this case, three successful hits meant they were certain of the animal tiring quickly.

The band of Jangwa chased the ill-fated boar, following its desperately loud and frequent squeals. This made it even easier to track, and now just ahead of them, they saw the dark brown back of the boar. It fought to pull its weight through the undergrowth with the detached arrows catching the small branches and shoots. As the hunters ran, all shouting excitedly, Fo made a rare mistake. He focused more on the boar he could see than the ground beneath him, for he had run along a secondary pig trail hoping to cut the animal off.

As he ran, both pig and hunters could be seen as they veered toward him. Suddenly - he was face first in the mud. A root had tripped him and he fell heavily, breaking two arrows and cutting his belly with a spear point, just below his bark chest protector.

Those who had seen Fo through the trees began to laugh as they heard the sound of him falling. Laughing while he ran, even Ukla was distracted and almost hit a small trunk protruding from the forest floor. Birds took to the air with the sound of the hunt. The forest was alive with sound when finally a hunter reached the boar, speared it in the abdomen and then struck its head with his adze. The hunt was finally over and they stood around, sweaty, panting and laughing excitedly at the euphoria the hunt produced. The laughing only increased as Fo limped into the clearing where they had dragged the dead boar, bleeding from his belly and carrying his broken arrows.

Fo was assisted with medicinal plants, chewed and applied to the cut, for they seemed aware of what iron could do if cut with it. It was a material strange to them but one they had adapted easily enough. It was scarce until more of the white peoples vessels washed upon the reefs.

The pigs of these islands were predominantly brown or black and that had surprised Ibo. He was used to a grey variety on his home island with their fur upon their backs made up of very stiff bristles. Usually a catch was skinned where it died, but this time they carried it home before gutting it and cooking it. Kue skulls were often hung as proud trophies of a hunt that always had potential to turn dangerous - should a frightened boar turn and charge in attack.

These Kue on Chiö-tá-kwö-kwé were an important part of their life for time immemorial. Very specific rules applied to hunting. No pregnant sows were killed and the oldest boars were left until they showed signs of weakness. The biggest were only hunted by individuals approaching the manhood ceremony, and no hunting was ever to occur during the time sows dropped their piglets.

By nature, these pigs were like all others. They bred twice a year and might have six to eight piglets at a time. This ensured a plentiful supply, but the Jangwa were careful not to over exploit. They treated all living things the same way. Their own children were born according to plenty or lack. Everything was ordered in the manner each generation was taught, and this had been occurring for thousands of years.

Roasting pork disturbed the spirits…so eating pigs could be a potentially dangerous thing to do. Yet this was part of the game of life as they all loved the meat, all sought it, all hungered for it. At the village, many others had already gathered. An aalaav was dug in the middle of the clearing and a fire lit some time before, now just a glowing mass of embers. Small stones were gently placed over the embers and a bed of leaves laid over those. The boar was disemboweled, stuffed with a certain leaf then the leg joints were partially cut before it was placed on the bed of leaves. They placed a thicker layer of leaves on top of the carcass, before the whole mound was covered in loose earth from the digging of the pit. This was different to some hunts where a killed pig was often cooked on a fire there and then, roasted openly and then cut up and the meat transported back to the camps. However, this was a special occasion for this was Po's opemame ceremony, and any excuse for a feast of well-cooked pork was always welcome.

As usual, stories were told during the feast, well…at least between long periods of silence at the beginning when all were busy stuffing themselves with as much as they could hold in their little bellies. But at the first hunt of the season, the same story was retold of a legendary figure of old, and a woman at that.

The story went that Timu-Le was a fearless hunter. She had been spoken of from generation upon generation going back way beyond their ability to comprehend. This was just as well because it was some thirty generations prior.

She had learned to use the bow as most children did, but at a time when few boys were being born. So skillful she became that she even participated in the defeat of a raiding party of fearsome Aka-bea-da. Never before had so many been repelled by so few. More than her own fingers, she had taken down with arrows; some even taken from the enemy she slew. For the Jangwa, like others, were not direct fighters in attack, but followed a hit and run tactic. Hide, fire arrows, run and hide again, all the while ensuring your aim was accurate, your enemy was harassed in unfamiliar territory, and ultimately defeated by a divide and conquer tactic. Of course, the Jangwa never attacked another tribe being limited to their own island and therefore always had the home advantage of knowing where tracks, outcrops and hiding places were.

However, Timu-Le had stood her ground, moving from tree to tree rather than fire and retreat. She was held in awe…and at a distance, once the enemy had left!

No one had ever done as she had done. Nor did they know how to handle this new situation for no woman had ever been so recklessly brave or so brazenly attuned to warfare. It was decided to send her on her own lepa, as boys would be before reaching adulthood. Girls had their own ceremony called opemame but Timu-le had participated in this the previous set of seasons when she gained her new name.

On Chiö-tá-kwö-kwé, only girls received a new name. After the great battle, she was classed as a great warrior in her own right, and now a skilled hunter. For she had returned from her lepa unscathed - forever placing herself as the prime story of wonder among Jangwa to this day. Women tended to have more authority among the tribes from that day on, especially in matters of fighting or when to hunting, although battles were seldom ever seen on this remote island.

Her lepa ended as she returned with not just one but two boar. These she had dragged back herself, one at a time to the beach camp, to the amazement of all. Of course, the stories may have been exaggerated a little but who could be sure - it was so long ago.

Beside Timu-Le, on the beach lay Tog, the legendary old boar that had evaded every individual hunter and had previously maimed two and killed one, in hunts from years past. For communal hunts were off limits as far as the oldest living boar was concerned, only during lepa could he be taken, and none had ever done more than pierced him with a single arrow.

Many surrounded the giant boar in awe and fingered his tusks and course back hair. Yet the greatest wonder was lying beside the old brown legend - a smaller white boar. No one had seen a white pig before or since.

All wondered how it could have evaded being seen until now. This was taken as a sign from the spirits, or even as a spirit. They debated to throw it into the sea but Timu-le would have none of it and she gutted it herself, handing the entrails and organs to any who dared eat it after she had partaken of some herself. They waited to see what would happen to her but nothing did. She seemed in full control and directed the men to cook it as well. But could spirits be killed? And if so, should they be eaten? "It is a gift," she said and went down to the beach to wash her hands.

Into the night both boar were cooked and feasted upon. Story telling began but all were kept short as it was the hunter's privilege to give his, or in this case, her account. Her description of the hunt was fascinating and her ability as a storyteller increased. Of course, the account may have been exaggerated, it even changed three times during the nights feast, but the key points never altered. It was she, who had hunted and killed them both - and on the same day.

Thus, Ukla ended his story, while many more began. Po was already in her special area marked by four upright stakes. Here she would stay for three days, her face covered in a special clay mixture. She would lie upon on a bed of belcum leaves over sticks of chik bag, the leaves of which menstruating women chewed. The belcum leaves were changed every morning.

While others feasted on the pork, she was offered nothing but the meat of a shelled sea creature and eeng. At the end of three days she bathed in the ocean, partook of some cold fatty pork portions, the fattier the portion - the better. The women in the camp gathered around and asked the spirits for a blessing of fertility while she was dressed in a string of leaves or kangape, and any flowers available at the time. Then the women would sing and their songs described what she would be required of her as an adult, children and how she would eventually ena-enga-le-ye with a boy from another family. The women said they would show her the two types of leaves used for preventing spirits placing a child within her. She then sang a song of her own, asking for blessing, children, and protection of the spirits. And at her own singing, all the men became silent as a mark of respect for her.

Not much changed in this idyllic existence…just a few wild storms and the occasional shaking of the land if the gods were angry. Some seasons were wetter, some drier but they followed the patterns as taught by the ancestors.

Ukla was fishing and a call went up from the beach. Immediately he poled the craft to shore.

"Strangers on the beach at Uiwa!" Fo said. "Not Onge', not Ung, but lighter skin," he said.

"Spirits?"

"No, but like those we have seen before, not spirit like."

The white stranger's made many visits from the sea but they had always hidden from them as best they could. Of course, there was the time they brought others with dark skin with them; they looked the same as the Jangwa but they no one understood what was spoken. No contact was made and they had always left the way they came. By the time the two reached the beach on the quiet side of the island down where the sun rises, a band of ten from that camp had completed the dispatch of the intruder.

He lay on his back on the sand, pierced with spears and his throat cut open like a pig. In the water, more of the things the dead man wore floated aimlessly in the sea. It appeared that two of these brown men had drowned in the waves, as a child had watched them at the reef edge. However, the third had managed to get to shore on a raft of bamboo where the others had attacked and killed him.

The raft intrigued them as they had never seen such a floating structure before and they dragged it into the bush. They left the dead man and returned to their village.

"He was afraid of us," Merebe said. "That showed us we were stronger," he laughed loudly as he described the pleas of the brown one before the first arrow hit. Four arrows in the abdomen he indicated. He then drew his hand across his throat. "Ilo-wa," he said indicating how he had dispatched him. Unlike other enemies, they did not dismember this body and did not bury it in the sand either as they still had uncertainty of the power that might be present in the bodies spirit.

So it appeared that the brown skins were easily killed then, the whites were probably not sea spirits but they did not understand the difference in color of the skin.

Three days passed and Foh saw yet another craft appear. Many men, all Ya-enga-Paluga-wa, were in their own smaller dange' and were approaching the beach.

Quickly he raised the alarm. He had them grab all they could from the temporary camp, load it into the four dange'. They then hauled them through the bush, before hiding them under branches and heading up the island to the new village. There, some twenty-four Jangwa now lived in eight shelters and huts. Foh had stayed close with Koko by his side, watching within the thick plants at the edge of the beach, close enough to see, far enough away to flee should they see him.

It always seemed strange that they covered themselves from head to toe and he was amazed at the colors, one similar to the flower of the e-dana-we. They gathered around the body, spending some time talking, but the language was very strange. Some carried the body to their dange' and the others ventured into the forest with the noise sticks Kanoi had described and warned about. They knew they could kill and he ran unseen from them to warn the village. But all fled, melting away into the trees along indiscernible paths they knew well, hiding in area of dense growth until all the stranger had left.

Once they had gone, various items of cloth and iron were found at obvious places of habitation. Other strange objects they didn't understand were also left, but these were discarded or if deemed usable by a spirit, buried.

The Blending

Koj was aware of the stories of the intense distrust between the Ung and all other tribes in those islands. Their hostility was the greatest of all the tribes. All Jangwa understood they were a people of the same ancestors, yet more closely connected to the Jangil. A delicate balance of life on the same island with the Onge and the Bea was mutual. The larger population of Bea on the north and west, kept the Jangil from attack until the brown ones and eventually the white man came and many of the Bea and Onge fell sick.

The Jangil could hide in the centre of the island well enough, but in time, they drifted back toward the coast. They were seeking others due to the eventual scarcity of contact with their neighbor tribes. The coastal villages were deserted, decimated and full of unusual items they had never seen before now. They talked with the few there and fled back into the interior.

Habia was one of few who ventured far from their traditional borders, always curious, always investigating always exploring, always learning.

Jereda had been the only one of his small village to go with the main group. Always at the rear, away from direct contact, he was nervous when he saw what had happened. He was even more fearful when those in neighboring villages began to get sick. He took his family deeper into the interior until their flight to Chiö-tá-kwö-kwé with some of their people, or so the stories told anyway.

However, in eighteen eighty-four, the British captured Habia and took him to Port Blair, being returned only when he became sick. Teela was Jereda's son and he followed what was passed down to him about the Embelakwe who also dwelt in the forest. Being Jangil, they were known as Engeakwe but they used to be coast dwellers once, like the Jangwa, but many generations ago.

So on that day, Koj met thirty-three Jangil, the last of them according to Teela, who arrived on the shores seeking refuge. They were not wanted on this island, and a brief fight ensued. Twelve Jangwa men and ten Jangil died in the process, so fierce was the skirmish. The woman Ek-Ana, a Jangil respected for her wisdom, managed to stop the fighting by using her loud shrill tone.

"A'ku gaibí," she cried. "We came to flee, not to die, nor to kill. Put down your weapons." The language was not Jangwa, but they could understand about half of the words spoken. All stopped, though none was in any mood to drop weapons. "Our ways are under threat and many die without battle. We came to seek refuge on *Chiö-tá-kwö-kwé* and offer our knowledge in return for safety here, a place more easily defended."

There was a murmur. She had called their island by the name they did. How did she know that they wondered?

Ek-Ana continued as best she could and explained the occurrences on their traditional lands, the white people, the death without weapons and the vision she had to flee and stay hidden forever. Then she looked at her husband and told him to put down his weapons. A bow length from him was one he had been fighting who held a spear, but regardless he dropped everything to the ground and kicked sand over it. Very slowly, all dropped their weapons and covered them in the sand. And so began an alliance, unseen by the wider unknown world.

The Jangil were a stronger people, produced better weapons and had learned to use iron they had found on the shores of their earlier home. They spoke an almost identical language and their ways were agreeable. Even the way they built their shelters appeared to be the same. The Jangwa knew nothing of the snobbery on other island between Embekwe and Engekwe as they would have called them.

"We know Dauwacho."

At that name, everyone fell silent. How could they know him they wondered?

"Drowned!" they said.

Yet Ek-Ana indicated she had met the man. Seemingly, he had managed to reach the east side of Gaubolambe where the Onge live. With him was a child. So now, the mystery was solved. They never knew what had happened to young Bo who disappeared one day - assumed drowned. Then it was Bo on the 'sep' with the Etobabu.

Dauwacho was banished from Chiö-tá-kwö-kwé for killing Ki. He took an old dange' and vanished over the reef, never to be seen again. Being an elder, he had been allowed to decide his own fate. Yet, in the end, he lived a life free of punishment.

"Is he...?"

"Dead?" she replied. "We heard Dauwacho had talked to the white people, a few Jangil said they met him and he was first to die of the sickness we are told. When sickness came with the white people, we fled from the coast to the forest and stayed there. The white people came with Aka'Bea guides to seek us out, but they never found us. Then some became sick and died. We lived in fear for a while but the rest of us are healthy. We decided to abandon our home and come here where we were told you have been successful in repelling the white people."

"White spirits of the sea!" Koj asserted.

"No, they are like us," she replied. "They are taller, hairier, they cover their skin. However, they bleed and they die. They carry more powerful, terrible weapons. They might look like spirits of the sea but they can be killed if their numbers are small enough."

Koj was not keen to accept any newcomers. He sensed that because these few managed to avoid any contact with the outsiders that killed those in the villages, they were clean. He approved their stay but directed them to an open area on the ocean side of the island to begin life. A watch was kept over them so Koj could see what the spirits did with them first.

However, within two weeks the sickness re-appeared. Koj understood an evil was present and they avoided the area for a long time until no more died. Four of his people died also. They buried all bones and things they had brought with them on the small island out from the shoreline. To ensure they would not turn into malevolent spirits, they performed all the rituals carefully, teaching the new arrivals how they did it on Chiö-tá-kwö-kwé. Koj believed that it was their isolation that kept them from the evil spirits that killed, and they vowed never to allow another living soul on the island of the Jangwa.

Few had ever been accepted, few ever chose to leave, and only one was ever been banished, sent on a canoe over the reef and east towards the Ung lands. It was assumed that if he ever made it, he would surely be killed. He had in fact reached Onge lands, being absorbed into the family that first met him on the beach.

Thus, the Onge and then the Jangil were once again reacquainted with the reality of the Jangwa legend as being true. The simple lean-to shelters were adopted as providing shelter, shade and breeze in a simpler and more easily constructed than their own round houses. With constant invasion by white and brown men, permanent shelters were becoming more infrequent. They cut their hair tighter and did not cover themselves with clay at night. Eventually these practices ceased with most Jangwa, except the women around the mouth and chin after marriage and they kept applying it for at least four seasons. Within a short time, even the length of hair was shortened as those Jangil began shaving heads as if it were normal. No one protested, and so the appearance of those on Chiö-tá-kwö-kwé began to change.

So, Teela lived, married and died on his new island home, learning the new ways but having the Jangwa trim their hair shorter at all times. He had worked for a few years to get at least something he felt was his own implanted in his new existence. It was not much, but he felt satisfied, as if it was the biggest victory of his life. On Chiö-tá-kwö-kwé, they could live as they did for years beyond count before the white man came, and it was easier to defend. And defend it they did.

Teela quickly assimilated to the life on this tiny island. It was so like his old home it became a little uncanny. He had learned from his home island that places with easy landing areas drew what they called the Ya-enga-Paluga-wa to their lands. But this place was harder to land at except at certain times of the year. He was pleased that all contact had met with fierce resistance and as his influence grew among the Jangwa, he cautioned the need to make sure this continued. For all he had seen and heard, was the white spirits brought death, one way or the other.

H was sure of something else…they could die! He had seen it himself years before when the Ung repelled what they also believed were white spirits at the time. You cannot kill spirits, but you can kill any human, no matter what color his skin and regardless of what he covers himself with.

It was this truth that made the Jangwa consistently aggressive towards those that would approach the island in the years to come.

From time to time both white and brown men reached their shores. Most were dispatched quickly; buried in the sand so none could find them. The Jangwa were not like the Onge', who would chop off the limbs of their enemies. They would dump the still living carcass in an open fire pit to rid them of the influence of evil spirits. Instead, the Jangwa buried any bodies to rot under the sand.

One craft with two brown men made it to shore only to flee when they saw the Jangwa appear out of the forest. Out of reach of arrows, they turned to see the natives unarmed and waist deep in the water and they were coaxed back with much gesturing until the two men, exhausted and thirsty made landfall.

They would discover, to their detriment, that the Jangwa had been dragging their weapons along with them underwater, with their toes. This trick had been taught by the Jangil who, strangely enough, were mostly forest dwellers in their history. This strategy allowed those on Chiö-tá-kwö-kwé to dispatch many an unwanted visitor and most of these deaths are unknown by the outside world.

Continuum

Long after Ukla had gone to the spirits and not long after his only surviving child N-agulemelegune had given birth to her first son, Taape-jagi-ya, much activity occurred in the sky and on the sea. The boy had been born in the early hours of a full moon, and over the sea, they saw bright lights and loud sounds carried across the waters.

They could not know that a bitter enemy of the Ya-enga-Paluga-wa had attacked from the air with weapons deadlier than they could ever understand. They had seen the noisy flying demons before, but not as if a swarm of insects and never as low as they flew around the island on this occasion. Had Chiö-tá-kwö-kwé been visited by those that now controlled Jara, and other islands, life may have been very different for everyone. The demons came across the reef one day and three Jangwa were ripped apart, in a way they had never before witnessed. Some unseen force shredded even the new dange'; small holes riddled the sides like the foga bug created in fallen logs.

The bodies were collected from the lagoon, buried; and the craft was covered in the underbrush. They fled to the interior of the island where they dwelt, abandoning the coastal camps for a long time.

In fear, they seldom ventured to the coast for fishing and only after cautiously checking the horizon for any signs of the dark demons of the sky. Occasionally in the distance, they could see them or the large dark eh-sep, as they were now called them. They only ever ventured out when nothing could be seen and nothing could be heard.

One of the many ancient abilities the Jangwa and others in similar islands had was the ability to taste or smell the wind. Temperamental spirits lived in the wind. The wind direction dictated where all Jangwa lived, what they hunted and what they gathered. Their entire culture existed around the direction and duration of the wind.

They could even smell a change coming. So, as the need to hunt pigs arose, the air would change, and the temperature cooled a little. They would then move into the forest areas of the interior, and invite the wind to come from where the vast open ocean lay slightly to the left of where the sun would sleep.

This wind they called Aholee-kwhade. The spirits that existed in the space above the forest moved about and so game was plentiful. But, if they made a mistake in observance of their many rituals, game may become scarce.

They painted their bodies with clay found on one side of the island and patterned by a chekwei. It could both release human scent or retain it, depending on what they coated themselves with. Always, the spirits were appeased to ensure longevity and health, both of themselves and the animals, plants and sea creatures they lived upon.

The rains started halfway through the pig-hunting season, ceasing only during the cicada season. Briefly, the rains returned in the turtle season, but only for about a single moon, not occurring again until halfway through the pig-hunting season once more. When some bright moons appeared after the winds died, it was again time for collecting the cicada grubs they craved. This cycle was never ending.

When the spirits in the wind started again, they came from the opposite direction. They called it Aahey-kwhade. At this time, they moved to the beaches in preparation for the time of the hard to catch turtles to be hunted. Turtle was a flavorsome meat. They were often tossed upside down in the fire still alive, and once again, this was done to appease the spirits.

The general idea was to be behind Aholee-kwhade and in front of Aahey-kwhade. All shelters are built between the two winds, but their main homes stood in one place and are encircled by winds and spirits that keep moving in and out of all things. They would change locations and avoid certain spirits and winds. This is the reason some encampments appeared abandoned when the Ya-enga-Paluga-wa appeared, for none were ever permanently habited.

In all their history, and even though the Jangwa had no concept of long lengths of time, no camp of shelter was ever placed in the same location as one previous. This was supposed to confuse the spirits. Even movement through the island's jungle, was most often done quietly and with as little trace as possible.

They knew the spirits were invisible to most Jangwa, but all knew they existed everywhere around them. As the spirits moved, the winds moved also, therefore the wind is the only expression, to most, of the movement of spirits. As one would move through the forest, plants would be touched by human hands and thighs. These would be cut down along the trails so they could not tell the animals where the Jangwa were moving to. So, as the plants feel the Jangwa, the presence of the spirits was felt by experience of the wind.

And so, it was once again time to frequent the coastal beaches. The island was just large enough that one could have lived in the interior permanently, but that would have created imbalance, both in health of the people, and in the health of that which they lived upon. So in fact, the traditions handed down for millennia served a perfect purpose.

This day, Pane-he' had his one surviving son, Omo-kabe, with him as he fished. The other older boy had died during their recent time in the forest of a snakebite that they could not cure in time. Pane-he' was aware the spirit of their dead boy might be lonely in the ocean and the sea would want to take the youngest brother also. Now, having moved back to the ocean temporarily, the risk had now increased. Omo-kabe therefore wore a string attached with shells with the occasional coating of clay for protection from the sun as it kept them cool. This practice seemed to be in decline compared to generations past.

The shells were tossed up from the ocean onto the sand, where as stones stayed in the depths due to their weight. The eneyetokabe that Pane-he' made his son wear represented, in miniature form, the anchor they used with a large stone on a cord, but shells were used because the sea returned those. This would keep Omo-kabe safe from the spirits of the sea's need to take him.

Quite often they could find a substance they called ele-ele. It was of similar feel to the le-mal in which the honey lived. It floated in from the ocean and some pieces as large as a skull could be found, or more often, as small as a fist. When small cut pieces were placed on a fire, a sweet aroma drifted through the village. Some would often put their head to the fire as a new piece was tossed in the embers, drawing a deep breath and moving back to his mat with a satisfied look on his face. In the outside worlds they knew nothing of, the amount they burned each year was worth a large fortune.

It was just near the end of the turtle season. The sea had been slight of late and due to a large feast the night prior, they were late getting to the beach just beyond the tree line. Out on the edge of the reef lay To-mahe-le-gele, a small island where some of the oldest bones of their ancestors lay. The spirit talkers would often go to this island. For many years, those on Chiö-tá-kwö-kwé would live and die as they always had. Many more ships would pass by and closer than before; some fishing just outside the reef and occasionally those that ventured further in to the bays were warned with a hail of arrows. Nevertheless, there had never been an actual confrontation and it seemed as if they would remain largely undisturbed.

For a very long time after n-agulemelegune's first son was born, frequent checks of beaches occurred. In some cases both in the morning, and in the evening. Over time, this practice had gradually fallen into decay. Therefore, it was that Wa-tá-jagi was to witness the beginning of a stage of contact that could have started the beginning of the end for the Jangwa - had it continued.

The dange' he was using only had a very basic outrigger they called meh, hardly the width of two fingers but it was enough, since a quick repair had been necessary. He would get around to repairing it properly another day.

An unusual noise caught his ears and he raised his head to be surprised by many men in a craft that suddenly appeared at speed into the lagoon. They were not Ya-enga-Paluga-wa or Eng-nga or even Ung. Taape-jagi-ya had heard the stories of another type of person called inenele-geru, and at first he froze, unsure of being caught in the open with two so young. He had nothing but a single bow and two fishing arrows. In a panic, he dropped his bow and picked up the pole, pushing them towards the shore as fast as possible. From the beach, two more dange' were dragged from behind the large fallen tree trunks and launched in response to Atah-jai's high pitched shrilling in his state of fear. For he had never seen any living creature outside that of his home.

Halfway to the beach, he stood up to signal those Jangwa coming out to them, slipped and fell awkwardly over the side and onto the meh, hurting his ribs in the process. Now underneath the craft he surfaced on the other side and grabbed the meh support than was strapped across the width of the dange'. Wa-tá-jagi stooped to place the bow inside the hull that he had recovered from the ocean in the commotion. Deeply Taape-jagi-ya pushed the pole into the sand and with much force, turned the craft toward the beach where the others had by now arrived.

Bows were drawn and several arrows fired toward the intruders as they shouted at them to leave. He knew they were not sea spirits, or so he had been taught over the years, but the whole situation was very disturbing. The young ones were frightened, as were the women, calling from the beach for all to return. By now Matea himself was on the beach. His bow had been handed down over many generations It was strong and very long and he fired a fishing arrow that was longer than his whole body far out towards the inenele-geru. It fell short, but not by much. However, the intruders seemed to have got the message as intended, retreating far out behind the reef where they sat for some time, eventually leaving well before the darkness finally fell.

Another two turtle seasons came and went. Fele was in the bay bounded by the island and the small peninsula. Hearing voices, he raised his head. There was no one else nearby, just a few children playing on the sand some distance away. The sound came again, this time a quiet deep thump thumping not unlike a hollow tree trunk being belted with a club. He raised his head to see some people in a brightly colored dange' of sorts. 'Was this what Taape-jagi-ya had seen last time?' he thought, as he stood transfixed at the sight as these brown men with covered bodies bore down upon him.

They waved at him, speaking in a tongue he could not understand. Being knee deep in water at the edge of the reef, there was nowhere to run. Some distance behind him was a basket with fish he had speared and he realized the extreme danger he was in, although he could not have known they would never have hurt him willingly.

Fitting a fishing arrow, for that is all he had; Fele aimed it at the inenele-geru who was within easy range.

Frantically they waved their arms and retreated a short distance away from the shore. Their hands were above their heads as they held something.

'Nariele!' he said to himself as he recognized the hard nut and lowered his bow slightly. The Jangwa craved these whenever they could be found as the sea gave them up to them. He was unaware of how these strangers could access these unless the sea gave them up to them also Suddenly a few were tossed his way; one was even lofted far enough to almost hit him. Landing with a splash in front of him, showering his face with seawater. Fele heard a laugh from one of the inenele-geru. 'So they laugh,' he thought and understanding something of the humor, he smiled in response. The inenele-geru witnessed a brief and very normal human response until his nervousness returned, and he raised his bow once again. They could see that the bowstring was not pulled as tight. There now began an awkward silence as all ceased speaking and stared silently at each other. Finally, Fele moved to gather the nariele, tossing them up onto the coral behind him, and then he turned and waded back up onto the coral exposed by the low tide. Gathering his fish basket, he placed as many of the precious nuts as he could into it and slung it over his shoulder. Turning toward the strangers, he raised his bow once more until they too turned away and moved out beyond the reef.

As he waded toward the beach, he watched as they continued around the small peninsula out of sight. Reaching the sand, he dropped his basket and sprinted through the small isthmus to see them continue around the island and out of sight.

"They arrive more often," Ten'elge said, as he pointed toward the ocean. More strange craft were appearing on the horizon than ever before. In the sky, strange noisy things passed through the clouds, and stories mentioned these things were not a traditional thing, but something new.

Change was occurring and all feared something terrible could happen sometime soon. The spirits were angry, and the surrounding activity suggested so.

Open Defiance

Along with their families, Go and Taape-jagi-ya were resting and talking to Foh who had appeared from the opposite shore the day before with his wife. It was the hottest part of the day and they lay in the shade of the trees. He had brought some of the sought after le to his favorite friends and they were enjoying the sticky sweetness under a basic lean-to shelter on the edge of the tree line.

Out at the reef, yet another colorful dange' appeared and headed in toward the beach. They were certain they could not be seen from where they sat, and so remained hidden, deep within the shadows. Foh reached for his bow but Go placed his hand on that of his friends, pushing the weapons back down.

"No, let us see," he said.

They waited as the inenele-geru stopped short of bow range, threw something overboard, immediately sitting down again. Occasionally they called out, but Go made everyone stay hidden in the shadows.

"They are offering us fish," Foh said with a startled tone. Indeed a type of fish they often saw but were too deep to shoot, were being held up. They were blue and green and their skin flashed in the sunlight. Foh stepped onto the beach before Go could prevent him. Now Foh was visible, Goh decided all would appear also, with weapons held at the ready. As the big fish were waved once again, Foh dropped his in the sand, covered them over and waded out into the ocean.

"Here," he urged. "Throw them here."

"What is he saying Mr Pandit?" one in the boat asked.

"I have no idea Dakshi," the anthropologist said, "But I'm sure they want the fish."

Foh waded out even deeper with arms raised, his hands indicating what he wanted. So the fish were thrown and Go and Taape-jagi-ya joined him in retrieving them, the biggest was as long as their outstretched arms. About seven large fish were tossed there way, and they were quickly dragged ashore by the grateful Jangwa.

"More, more!" they called, "But do not come ashore," and they threatened with gestures and spears, but they had no understanding of what the inenele-geru were saying in reply. The dange' came closer with its strange thumping noise, like a drumbeat. In response, they raised their bows and pointed arrows at the strangers. This made them turn around but stay close enough so they could still see each other clearly.

Suddenly a woman grabbed Foh and pulled him aside, put his weapons on the ground and sat in his lap in a tight embrace. Foh was aware that his wife wanted them to calm down. All the women grabbed their husbands and did the same whereas the growing tension eased.

This practice was a form of greeting after a long journey, an embrace before leaving for a journey, or just a social expression where it was impossible to be angry for long. The

Jangwa, as did those of other tribes in those islands, had practiced this for many millennia. All humans know that touch diffuses tension.

In a short time, others arrived from elsewhere on the island. They stood guard in the trees, some as high as twenty feet off the ground, weapons in hand, watching in case they were needed. For this was Go's home, and they deferred to his leadership when here. And it was he that seemed unconcerned about those in the dange' drifting quietly closer towards shore.

Now some smaller fish were offered, and this time the children waded in to retrieve them. No words were spoken. To Go and those with him, this seemed less threatening than words they could not understand. After a short time, the visitors turned around, retreating to the open ocean. Out beyond the reef they could see a larger eh-sep and they watched as the dange' was lifted up into it and disappeared around the island and out of sight.

Over the years, visits became frequent enough for the Jangwa to know when and where the inenele-geru would appear. Always their beloved nariele were left in a strange woven bag. Hollow containers were sometimes left but they were not made of anything they knew, was not unlike the hard substance sometimes found attached to driftwood. Water did not seem to affect this material.

On one such visit, the strangers came very close to the beach. A few arrows were fired and Matea actually scored a direct hit on one of them, right in the leg. He danced for joy at the sight as the boat now left the lagoon.

"Come back and we kill you," he shouted in jubilation as they left.

Over time, consistent visits occurred, and they began to recognize one of the strangers as the same person. At every occasion they were rebuffed, often arrows were fired and sometimes they just insulted them by pretending to defecate. It seemed to work as Ale' noticed as each time they did it, the strangers left soon afterward.

There was one day where Matea and four others did not reach the beach before the strangers arrived, and on this occasion, a kue had been secured to a stake in the sand. Its color and skin was strange although they knew what it was, but they just speared it and buried it in the sand, before dragging the bag of nariele away into the forest. The strangers drifted offshore but just out of reasonable reach of arrows. No one sent off a warning shot – that would have been wasteful.

The seasons came and went and life continued as it had before. Much discussion revolved around the strangers, their lack of aggression, and what should be done about them. After all, they did bring them nariele and things that would hold water yet were impossible to break.

These kwentale, as they now called the strangers, were not wanted on their island, yet time made the Jangwa less afraid. They were aware of the stories of old from those who had come from where the Jangil once lived.

"We must not let them come here," Taape-jagi-ya insisted.

"But we cannot stop them coming here," Bea-ne' pointed out the obvious.

"This is true Bea-ne', but they must not land. If their foot lands their body will follow; if their body lands, our lives will change."

"But they bring gifts," Leiale stated, although this was no revelation to anyone. Opposite the fire sat some brightly colored containers, although two had split already.

"For what purpose? No, we must resist!" insisted Matea, who now waded in on the debate. "We must prevent them standing on the land at all costs."

"But they bring no harm, do they"? Bea-ne' asked.

"You are young Bea-ne'. You do not know all the stories. These are not like the Ya-enga-Paluga-wa - this is true. We have not seen one for a very long time, almost since before I was born. These are kwentale; we were told they used to come with the Ya-enga-Paluga-wa but not as ones of dominance. But where are they now? Did the Ya-enga-Paluga-wa leave, or did the Kwentale kill them all?"

No one answered for they could see he was not finished speaking, so they waited.

"From the Ung lands the Jangil came and told us what happened to the Onge when Ya-enga-Paluga-wa came. No - they must be repelled."

"Nariele."

All conversation stopped. Bea-ne' had just named what they loved to eat. It was true when the Kwentale came they brought many nariele.

"Then we take them and force them away. We take what we want, we decide - not they!" he decided, standing and wandering off, leaving the rest to discuss the nearness of the honey season.

The next few days brought a storm into the region. They were already inside the forest as the winds started. The storm was both sudden and earlier than anticipated for the season change, and when it finally cleared, a large vessel appeared, wedged firmly on the outer reef. This was a repeat of what had already happened further down the windward side some years earlier.

They watched from the shoreline for some time for they had been collecting the hard substance for their arrows and spear points from the previous wreck but this one was different. On this one, they could see inenele-geru moving about onboard.

Once the weather improved, dange' were launched and they tried to get out on the reef but capsized in the waves. All managed to get to shore safely but they were shaken; both with the size of the wreck and their near death experience. One bow and a number of arrows were lost in the capsize. Yet another 'eh-sep' came and they could clearly see an attempt to draw close by, but that too failed due to the raging seas.

When the weather finally cleared and the swells subsided, the Jangwa were able to draw nearer and came alongside metal hulk wedged on the reef. The fired a few arrows at the heads looking over the side, but there was no way to climb up the slippery sides and they finally abandoned the attempt after seeing the futility of it. From a distance, they stayed hidden and observed, until a frightening sight appeared in the form of a large and noisy dragonfly. It appeared geru in color like the ones of the forest, and landed and took the men off and another some days later. This terrified the Jangwa and they hid in the forest while it hovered. They could not imagine what it was, or why it consumed men the way it did, but they took it as a sign that the spirits were angry at the inenele-geru.

Over the dry season's the kwentale would continue to come and take pieces from the eh-sep and so did the Jangwa, for iron became a useful tool for spear and arrow tips. They kept their distance, sometimes drifting near to stare but never getting close enough as suspicion was rife on both sides of the cultural divide. A number of times those that got close were injured and two were killed suddenly by something making a loud noise and they avoided those working on the large hulk on the reef after that.

In time, they saw the same kwentale they had seen in the past. Once again, the usual gifts were left. Each time they managed to get closer to the beach unhindered, always guarded, but with no real sign of aggression outside of the usual posturing.

Foh had since died, and Matea now had more influence over the groups on the island. He had a plan to ensure these strangers left them alone forever but he told no one. Most were surprised at the lack of anger he displayed whenever the familiar kwentale arrived in their dange', and today was no exception.

The camp filled with Jangwa due to the lack of wind and the beginning of the honey season. Most were finishing a feast of it when the familiar sound interrupted their seclusion. There were twenty-eight Jangwa at the camp this day and all rose to their feet, grabbed their weapons and looked to Matea. Slowly he stood and silence enveloped him as a quiet fear and determination swept through him.

"Put them down," he said waving his hand to reinforce his words. "Let them come."

With much trepidation on their part also, the kwentale brought their boat to a depth of only half a meter. Here the little black bodies of the Jangwa were able to collect the coconuts thrown to them and even take one from the hands of a kwentale. A sudden movement startled Nila. A very fat visitor leapt out of his craft and into the ocean up to his chest with a nariele in hand. The action caused him to panic but Matea saw his opportunity and disappeared into the foliage to recover his bow.

"No!" A voice came from behind him.

Turning he saw his wife. "No", she repeated and forced his hands down. They watched together in the shadows as the stranger gave out many nariele to the many Jangwa who surrounded him in the water. Then they watched him climb back aboard and he left the bay. Matea noticed the one who seemed to be their leader, was not present on this occasion.

"We missed an opportunity to prevent them coming anymore Keje," he said to his wife. "How did you know?"

"I watch", was all she said, and they joined the others to break open and feast on the white flesh and liquid within the gifted nuts.

It seemed like just a few days had passed when the same craft with its strange noises, appeared once more. Most had stayed at the camp, still in honey collecting mode. This time the one they recognized from most previous visits was present. Once again, Matea encouraged all to leave their weapons behind, although their adzes were still in their belts. Matea could hear them talking, but had no idea what about.

"Dr Pandit!" the accompanying policeman called. "Do you plan to enter the water?"

"Yes, I do, why?"

He patted his rifle, "Just in case."

"I do not think that is necessary, and only if I say... and only fire in the air. We are in their home now Ranjit, you would defend yours I believe?"

The policeman nodded in understanding. He accompanied most of these trips. He too was sympathetic to the cause of protection of these islanders. This time Matea led the entry to the water. He was curious, yet ever fearful. What would he learn, what would they do? Soon, some fifteen Jangwa were surrounding the boat taking the bags of nariele offered to them. The man they recognized, who wore something strange on his face, entered the water and immediately became surrounded by a mass of smaller black bodies. They could hear the kwentale talking to one another.

"Mr Pandit?" the policeman asked in concern.

"I am fine, they are curious that's all," he said as his glasses were taken off, never to be seen again. Others joined him in the water. Again the policeman asked an opinion of Dr Pandit as Jangwa started to climb into the motorized dingy.

"Stay put, they are only curious," he urged.

Bea-ne' was one of those aboard and he saw a strange item lying in a corner and reached out to touch it but was startled with a slap to his hand. This offended him and he jumped out into the sea again.

Quite some time had passed. All the nariele had been taken; some clothing and other small items and the Jangwa were now ready to see the visitors off.

As Matea watched, only the familiar one who he assumed was their leader was left in the water. He fingered his adze but his eyes drifted toward the shore as he heard a familiar voice call his name. Keje had been following him closely. Her influence over him was strong and she cautioned him.

"No Matea, leave him alone, let him go. They have brought us gifts and some che, and they show no aggression," she said. "And look..." she continued, "I have these!" She waved something in her hand and he left the water to see what it was.

She handed him what the main Kwentale was wearing on his face. Matea fumbled around trying to get them on and when he finally did, he just grunted and threw them on the sand, "Ah, they hurt my eyes," he said, as things went blurry. Keje quickly stooped, picking them up. For she had noticed she could see clearly through them and she proudly kept them on for many, many days until they finally were lost somewhere in the jungle, much to her annoyance.

While in the water, the anthropologist found himself surrounded by the islanders and closer to the shore and than he was to the safety of his boat. An aggressive act by Atah-jai, in drawing a blade and pretending to poke the anthropologist's chest, made him call for help. The boat quickly turned around, its motor and sudden action scattering the remaining Jangwa and allowing Dr Pandit to get safely aboard.

Nila laughed at the panic Atah-jai had caused. He was aware that they could have slaughtered them all if they had wished. The nariele were a welcome gift, as always. Matea sat on the sand on his haunches examining the incident. There had been no aggression, they seemed friendly, they offered gifts, they came regularly and the same ones each time.

A familiarity had therefore softened the Jangwa toward these strangers and he was beginning to wonder if they should encourage them onshore. 'At least they could be killed easier,' he mused although this was more to justify his first thought. Keje came to him and sat in his lap and they embraced and remained that way for some time.

"There they go again Dr Pandit," said Ranjit, "Are they mating?"

"No," said the Doctor who now had a spare set of spectacles adjusted to his face. "It's just a form of calm and solace I think. It seems to settle them, and if they have been in trepidation of our visit then this may be their way of calming down their nerves," he said, recalling all his observations over the years.

"See?" Keje provoked, "No danger!" But Matea did not reply. His thoughts were on what could go wrong if they allowed the kwentale on their homeland. For many generations, stories had been told of invaders, and what happened to the likes of Nali, Kanjoy and Kanjo who returned unharmed. Also Fo and Asi who died at the place of the Ye-enga-Paluga-wa. Their children returned, but three died shortly afterward.

But all that had come since, as the stories told, were repelled, and the spirits seemed less troubled, or so it appeared. The stories still seemed to change over time as far as Matea could recall. He was sure as a child he had heard them told differently... 'ah, but I was a child,' he said to himself. He swiftly dismissed the thought, returning his attention to the new arrow tip he was shaping from the hard substance obtained from the crumbling shape on the reef.

Upheaval

Two full sets of seasons had come and gone. The kwentale had only returned once more in that time. Three new boys and two girls had now been born at this end of Chiö-tá-kwö-kwé where Atah-jai lived. He knew of the visits and had seen many on the edge of the reef fishing but none had ever come ashore that he had seen.

He delivered his son to Matea's camp at the marriage of Matea's daughter to Ke. Faaste, his younger brother, also asked to live at this end of the island. From here the southeast winds came, signaling the pig season and time to live deeper in the forest. But for now, it was honey season, and they were again in the coastal camps.

Here, for the first time, he saw the kwentale up close and personal. As they approached in the same craft he had seen on the edges of the reef near his village, his excitement grew. Without thinking, he plunged into the water and waded out to the boat where a brown man smiled at him as he took something off his face.

Atah-jai grabbed the front of the craft and began to pull it toward the shore. He heard the chatter of those in the bright dange' but he could not understand what they said, but the man still smiled at him.

Slowly the craft of the kwentale was gently pulled toward the beach, closer than any had ever been in this bay.

"What is he doing," Matea asked, surprised at Atah-jai's actions. "I don't want them on our home," he asserted.

Keje put her hand on his shoulder. He knew to say nothing else, and he got up and walked away. As he did, he picked up his bow and a few arrows and retreated into the shadows to watch. Keje followed him there to ensure he provoked nothing.

Although nervous herself, she remained a curious woman and liked to see what would happen when certain things arose. Such as when a few seasons back, an unexpected heavy rain had arrived early while they were still on the coast, and with the winds and sideways rain, the campfire died. They were horrified to find their precious fire store had also been extinguished. Lack of fire for those who were intent guardians of it was potentially disastrous. They left immediately to travel into the interior of the island to the other villages to find fire. They would bring it back using a tuhi-ga, a resin soaked bundle of tied leaves they often used at night for fishing.

Keje was an attentive observer of the goings on at the beach in recent years. She observed one of the kwentale use a small colored thing to light a small pile of dry leaves. It had been discarded as they always had fire so there was never a need to use something else. However, Keje had retrieved it, used it occasionally, always amazed at how the flame came to life and stopped when her finger released the thing that would move at the top. Taking it to a tree hollow she found a handful of dry leaves and began a fire, bringing it back to the shelter when the rains subsided. And after dark, a tired Matea and three others returned with a lit tugi-ga to find fire already burning inside the shelter, much to his amazement.

So here she stood, beside her husband as his fingers held a loosely fitted arrow to his bow. He dare not do anything else while she stood beside him, and they watched what unfolded on the sand of the beach.

Dr Triloki Pandit was the first to leave the boat, deciding that at this point they had no option but to trust the little black islanders that swarmed around them. He ordered the motor cut. The policeman, always present on these trips, questioned the wisdom of this, but complied when he saw having a motor running would do little good if the bow of the boat were beached on the sand, at what was now high tide.

As the anthropologist slowly left the safely of the boat, hands once again pawed at his body. His skin color and abundant hair fascinated everyone. He placed a sack on the sand, stooped to open it and reached inside to reveal a sought after treat. Nariele were always gratefully received, and he produced a few metal pots, and a gift none had seen before.

Atah-jai was the first to take it and clamp his teeth on what was indicated as something to eat but he drew back his mouth in disgust as all the kwentale laughed. The first man who came ashore they already had a name for, Pante', they called him, as the best they could pronounce what they thought he called himself or what he was. Pante' became the only kwentale ever given a name. He took the item and pulled off a covering, exposing a brown soft substance, and handed it back. Atah-jai did not like the taste although others around him did, and the chocolate bar disappeared along with a dozen more as quickly as they could be produced.

They escorted Pante' toward the shelter where a fire continually burned. Only two others came with him from the boat the rest stayed there, including the policeman who fingered his rifle out of sight.

All three were stripped to their waist but Pante' had gone further, undressing completely. His nakedness was why the Jangwa trusted him more, for he tried to appear as they were. Ke was fascinated at this stranger even more so than Atah-jai and he clung to Pante's arm like a long lost friend.

Matea watched from the shadows not liking much of what he saw. "Be calm, be quiet," Keje said as she patted his chest. "Settle inside. Do not fear. I have good feelings about this," she said in reassurance. At that, he relaxed and he lowered his weapons to his side but refused to leave his hidden vantage point.

Pante' then pulled out a large piece of pork and presented it to them. "ön-a-bo," they chanted. So at least they saw something they recognized and liked, but its pre-salted taste created some strange facial effects. "Kue," they called it and Pandit recognized the name as being the same as the Onge word for a pig, for indeed it was. Most other words were a mystery.

To Pandit, the islanders talked so fast, and with such a shrill, that it was hard to distinguish anything at all. The clamor of the meeting could be heard out beyond the reef, as the ship MV Termugli stood by. Many on board stood at the railings, binoculars in hand, intently watching all that was unfolding. They were a little surprised that the doctor had been so easily welcomed ashore. Finally, Matea himself appeared out of the shadows with Keje at his side.

The excited chatter of the Jangwa suddenly ceased. The strangers were now aware of a slight tension in the air. Matea saw their eyes examine himself and his wife and then the long bow he carried. He saw a slight hint of fear in their eyes and it pleased him. He continued to hold their gaze as if as if they were the enemy and the first to budge would be defeated. Of course, he couldn't do it as well as Keje, but it worked nonetheless because now, the one they called Pante' lowered his eyes, sensing the need to do so.

This made Matea laugh and he handed his bow to his wife and strode forward, fingering the visitor's hair and skin, pleased at their nakedness instead of those ridiculous coverings they always wore. Taking his arm, he towed him through the camp describing how they lived and what things were.

While one kwentale showed the natives a box of matches, Matea managed to get the one they called Pante' into the forest and on the well-worn paths. Here, away from the others, Matea had a chance to finally take action and kill the one he had wanted to for so long. However, his intention was distracted when the stranger pointed up into the canopy. There, bees buzzed around the beginnings of a new hive.

Matea laughed again as this was one they had not noticed, yet it was so close to camp. He slapped Pante' on the buttocks and grabbed his arm, pulling him back to the others having decided that these people were good, not bad and they should be allowed to visit.

Those around Pranab had initially been unimpressed with the matches, after all, the fire did not last long at all compared to their resin torches, and ones hand became burnt if it was held for long. Even after demonstrating their use on a few dry leaves, they shrugged. One went to the nearest hollow tree and revealed their own source of embers by which to light a fire, should the one in the shelters go out.

For three hours, they mingled around the huts until a sound came from what waited outside the reef. The ships horn suddenly made the kwentale stand up and move toward their dange' on the beach. The Jangwa were not so keen to let them leave as they clung to them, stroked them, and chatted furiously and smiles spread from one side of their little black faces to the other. Finally, they climbed aboard their craft and left, but there was much sadness on the part of the islanders as if they were losing someone they would never see again.

Unfortunately for Dr Pandit, once he arrived at Port Blair, advice came that no more visits were to be made to the island. Unbeknown to the Jangwa, this was the last they would ever see of those they had become to trust enough to have contact and in time they became suspicious of outsiders once again.

It was now many years since the kwentale had been forced to stop visiting.

Atah-jai could remember an incident from the past where a sudden inability to stand occurred, as the ground moved beneath him wildly. The noise that seemed to come up from the very earth itself. The movement like a roaring wave, and with the violent swaying of the giant trees, myriads of birds took to the air in a noisy protest at being disturbed. Three kue had run close by, almost oblivious to his presence as they scurried off in fear, more concerned with the ground that shook than the man in their way. He had stumbled and fallen with the surprise of the shaking and his turning to see the pigs flee. For some time the shaking occurred, with a disorientating sideways movement. Just as suddenly as it arrived, the swaying stopped and the sound disappeared, as if like a wind into the distance. He had quickly returned to the camp where they were already collecting possessions, ready for moving up to higher ground. The tide was full and lapped the golden sand not far from the closest lean to shelter on the beach. Yet not even that shelter had been touched by the water surge that often came with these events.

However, this early morning was different. The forest, already alive with the chatter of birds, erupted as they took to the skies in a loud and raucous gathering just before it shaking hit. The sound was deafening, but the ground did not sway as usual, but shook as if cold and in need of warmth. He could stand slightly better than before as he gripped a tree buttress and held on tight. On and on the shaking went and the ground could be seen to move, and in places, crack along the limestone outcrop near the beach. So relentless was the movement, he had to cower between the huge buttresses as branches fell and leaves littered the air like rain. Insects swarmed on the surface as he had never seen before, and the ground continued to heave and the sound became louder still.

Crashing sounds came from within the forest. He feared what creatures may have come until he saw with his own eyes, a large tree falling across the track not far from where he crouched in fear. 'What could the spirits be so angry about that the trees fell before them,' he wondered. From the beach not far away, other strange sounds occurred and he could hear screams from the women and even some of the men. Still the ground shook as if the spirits were trying to return all men to themselves. Eventually, even he covered his ears with his hands as he leaned against the giant tree and waited for his life to end.

Finally a silence came. Only the birds could be heard, reeling high in the sky. Slowly raising himself to his feet, he saw the forest floor littered with debris from the canopy above, and heard a buzzing near his head. A bee's nest had fallen along with an old branch and he fled them as he raced toward the beach. What he saw when he arrived amazed him even further.

The lagoon should have been full of water. Instead, rocks appeared everywhere as if the tide was out, yet the level of the reef seemed higher than before. His mind could not comprehend what had occurred and his attention was diverted to the trees that littered the beach. Even the shelters used by his family lay flattened. Everyone, wa-tá-jagi included, was busy - hurriedly collecting his or her tools and weapons.

Taape-jagi-ya was an old man by now, but his words were now ringing in their ears as they gathered all they could to flee inland. They moved toward the highest point Chiö-tá-kwö-kwé could offer, before the sea came to claim them. Atah-jai could now remember the stories of waves entering the forest, but he had never seen it occur.

Even the old man had a look of fear on his face and he disappeared inland as quickly as his old legs could carry him. Everyone from the northern parts of the island headed to the sanctuary on the highest point on the island. This high point was near where Matea's camp lay to the south. At this spot, close to the sea, the land rose sharply to the gentle ridge where they would be safe.

All the same, a few curious boys ventured down toward the beach to have a look. Ahme and Faatse were inseparable friends and while some eighty-five people took refuge together, these two got bored waiting, sneaking away with two more friends down toward the shoreline.

The beach appeared much the same, with a few fallen trees, but the reef looked very different. Much of it protruded through the water, and they all knew that the tide should be high, and as such, this did not feel right. Directly in front, where the long reef lay just out from the beach, the reef was exposed and ran a long distance just along and parallel with the shoreline. Out toward the open ocean, the little island that usually stood amid water on all sides, now stood proudly exposed on a shelf of rock or reef. It appeared to have been raised up the height of a full-grown man. Once a deep bay, now it was as shallow as where the wreck on the reef lay at the opposite end of Chiö-tá-kwö-kwé.

Faaste became scared at the sight. "The spirits are angry," he said. "We should leave."

But Ahme seemed unconcerned.

"It has been a while, and look - no waves," he said.

Unconvinced, Faaste, along with Sik-me and Ohet, began to climb back to a place of safety where they could look between the trees. The forest was thick here where the winds created a permanently bent canopy, so they climbed a rara tree where the ocean and the reef could be clearly seen.

From their vantage point, they could see Ahme as he walked out upon the reef a short distance. He stooped to retrieve a fish he spotted, thrashing in a small pool of water. Out of the corner of his eye, Ohet noticed something happening at the edge of the reef where the water boiled and suddenly dropped away, the bay draining even more so with it.

Urgently they cried out to Ahme, who observed the change himself and he turned to run back to the safety of the trees. Reaching the sand, he glanced over his shoulder to see a huge wall of water rising above the reef. His friends now screamed wildly, urging him to run for his life, and he turned to run back up the slope. Scrambling through the tree line, he climbed the slope toward where his friends perched on a branch high above the ground. He panicked when he could hear a loud crashing as the waves entered the forest below him. Ahme was in the lowest branches, not quite as high as Sik-me and his friend, and he reached down to Ohet's outreached hand as he saw blackened water surge up the slope.

Ahme screamed in terror, almost slipping but managing to grasp Ohet's hand, and he pulled him up to the branch he was sitting upon. The surge of water continued and Sik-me and Faaste watched in horror as the blackened water engulfed their friends and surged further up the slope. They were aghast at its force and speed. After all they sat at least two dange' lengths off the ground and quite a distance up the slope. As the water receded, the branch Ahme and Ohet had been holding onto was empty and they could barely see Ohet being dragged back down the slope with the water as it returned to the sea. Finally managing to grab a smaller tree trunk, he held on exhausted, unable to move due to injuries sustained from being bashed by debris and from hitting trunks of trees in the first surge. They could see blood that began to pour from his head.

"Where is Ahme?" they yelled above the sounds of the water receding across the reef. All Ohet could manage was to shake his head, as he did not know, and had no energy with which to speak. However, the sound was not the water withdrawing, but yet another wall bearing down on the island. They watched again, aghast, as Ohet was again engulfed and swept up the slope and then dragged down again, his screams for help silenced by the noise.

Back at the village, a few adults noticed four boys were missing and went in search of them, tracking them to the point where they heard screams. They stood at the point at which Ahme and Ohet disappeared. Waiting to be sure than no further surges would occur they retrieved Faaste and Sik'me and returned with them to the camp.

The following day they launched a search. They would never see Ohet again, although Ahme's body was found; wedged in branches nearer the shoreline. The devastation was astounding. Large trees were torn from their place of sentinel, rocks, fish, coral, and creatures so strange they feared them, littered the beaches around the island.

They buried Ahme according to custom, and the northern clan ventured back to the wide bay to the north. The waves had savaged the shoreline. With lower lying lands and a small area of swamp, the surge had ripped apart everything in its wake.

No remnant of any Jangwa hut or dange' remained in sight, although finally one craft was found far inland undamaged. Eventually two more were found but smashed beyond any form of possible repair. Once again, strange creatures never before witnessed, lay dead upon the reef. One or two were still alive in shallow pools, unable to return to the depths from where they had been rudely thrown. These they speared and left to die. They would eat nothing unfamiliar, or that connected to the spirits of the sea. The large seashells they desired lay scattered everywhere and they even found dead turtles in the bush.

They explored the area to see what else had occurred. Sacred sites such as at the peninsula had been destroyed. The whole landscape of the shoreline lifted, and the corals died and began to stink.

Other strange objects lay on the reef. Colored containers of a material they were familiar which appeared. On the reef at the bottom of the island, lay four large hard objects. No one knew what they were or how to open them, but they made a loud hollow noise when struck. It appeared they were built of che, the same material as the wreck on the reef, from which they made points for their arrows and spears.

For three days after the sea surge, they slept on higher ground. Only a few cautiously ventured down to the beaches to examine the damage. When the frightened ones arrived at the beaches, they were astonished at the sight of the reef being exposed and the uprooted trees scattered around the beach and reef. With dange' gone they now had no means of fishing in anything but knee-deep water.

Many days later, as they gathered around the area the called Maa-kwé, a heavy and disturbing sound filled the air. From around the island another flying demon appeared. In the past, they had hovered like the dragonfly above the now rusting hulks on the reef, now scattered further with the recent tsunami. But this day, the hovering demons advanced directly toward them. Many feared they were about to be taken and screamed in terror.

Quickly Maabea fitted an arrow to his bow and let it fly, coming close but to the left of the demon. He was sure he could see a kwentale inside, and he questioned why those he had seen many years before as a child would now be inside these flying demons. Were they captured? And why come here so soon after the spirits of the sea had raged so much? At that thought, he fitted another arrow and watched it fly overhead and then back again toward the open sea as other Jangwa arrived and fired more arrows. By now Maabea was joined at his side by others approaching from the forest edge. The attack seemed to work as the demon stayed only a brief time, before heading over toward the land of the Ung.

The quakes disturbed the Jangwa in ways no outsiders would ever understand. No story was remembered of the extent of the spirits anger they had just experienced. They remained afraid; aware the flying demon was linked to the ground shaking and eventually convinced that the shaking was linked to the lack of visits by the peaceful kwentale of years before.

Much discussion followed around the fires and all decided that no visitors would ever be allowed on the island again as best as they could repel them.

Soon afterward, two more ground shakings convinced them this was the right course.

Yaketa (day after tomorrow)

Those on Chiö-tá-kwö-kwé remained nervous and suspicious after the events at the end of the wet seasons two years before now. They camped all along the coast because now the wind had taken the spirits into the forest. Although the giant waves had taken or broken their dange' and they had made a few more to replace them. However, they needed much more work to be as good as those they previously used.

Matea now took charge of the entire island. No clear leader or chief had ever existed. The idea never even entered their heads, but his outspokenness banded them together. After the spirits shook the ground, his voice became not just the loudest, but also the most insistent.

Maabea was also a feisty one but deferred to Matea in almost all matters but the kwentale. It was he who was even more determined that any soul landing on their home should die. And it was Maabea who, early one morning, saw a kwentale craft drifting in the lagoon on the higher tide. From outside the reef there were two more of these craft and men were standing up and shouting toward shore for an unknown reason. No one could be seen in the floating craft from where Maabea stood, but he quietly called for his sons to come with him.

They waded out to the craft floating in waist deep water. Inside two kwentale appeared either dead or asleep. Maabea spoke to his youngest son to raise the alarm and he left reaching shore and ran into the forest toward the village. "Have an arrow ready," he instructed his son. "If they stand up – kill them," he said to Tale' as he prodded the bodies lying in the bottom. They stirred and made a noise but did not wake.

Maabea did not know why, but he assumed they were in hullu, as they looked like they were overcome with fever. Again he prodded the bodies and one stirred from his slumber to come face to face with a reality he had not planned. The man lashed out and grabbed the end of Maabea's bow, wrenching it from his hands and leaping to his feet. The act stunned both the stranger, who was not quite awake, and Maabea, who stumbled back to the sand in shock at having his bow taken by someone from his very hand. In sudden anger, he pulled his axe from his belt and threatened the kwentale who by this time was shouting in obvious fear to his companion.

"Raj!" he called, as he shook his friend vigorously. "Get up, the islanders are here," he yelled but there was only a slight stirring. He picked up a hooked pole and swung it at the small black man in front of him, yelling at both him and Raj, still stirring in the bottom of the boat. Maabea was close enough to be struck, but managed to duck in time and ran back up the beach calling into the forest for help, which soon arrived.

To their horror, the fisherman watched as no less than a dozen armed islanders stormed out onto the sand, all calling and yelling to each other. They were obviously angry and gestured toward the kwentale to leave and aimed arrows at them. The fishermen failed to get the engine started and during this frantic attempt, Raj managed to stand up, instantaneously receiving an arrow that pierced his abdomen and appeared out his back. Screaming in pain and from the shock, he fell to the base of the boat as Tiwari frantically tried to start the engine, which finally spluttered to life.

By now, many more Jangwa descended on the beach and four were already pulling the edge of the boat and preventing it from leaving. Tiwari took a knife and pointed it menacingly at Mue' who was the closest, but a single arrow entered his chest. He fell overboard, and was set upon by more from the beach who dragged him from the water and hacked him to death with their wohen.

Raj could hear his friend's screams until silenced, and he cried out in realization of his death. Raj was also dragged, kicking and screaming to the sand, blood pouring from his belly wound and staining both sea and beach a dull red. He wriggled free of those holding him and staggering wildly he tried to escape down the beach. There was never any hope of escape but all he wanted to do was distance himself from the natives. When another arrow appeared through his chest he looked down at the bloody point protruding over a hand width out the front from a well-aimed shot to his back, he began to cry. Falling onto his knees, he waited for the final blows to come.

Matea watched as the final stranger was dispatched, and they celebrated the defeat of those who dare approach their island without invitation. Some speared them further, and then they quickly dug a shallow hole, moving both bodies into the slight depression and hacking them more before covering them with sand.

"Look," cried Tali as he pointed out into the lagoon. The dange' the kwentale had arrived in was moving toward the ocean, making the same noise they made when they moved so rapidly. They could not understand how it could move without anyone aboard but they kept watching until the colored craft grounded itself on the reef as the tide went out. The sound continued to be heard throughout the day until it finally stopped, just as night fell. The incoming tide washed it firmly on the exposed reef, raised higher since the earth had moved so violently.

Many strange objects had washed up on the reef in recent times. Strange large solid containers one of which was full of strange things they had no understanding of, once they had worked out how to open them. Over time, weather, tides and waves spread these items all over the reef edge.

Two days had passed and the village heard a deep thudding sound like a stick on a large hollow tree.

"The demons," screamed Tila to Maabea who rushed out onto the beach from their shelters.

The flying demon hovered high above them and once again, they saw human forms inside. Immediately they began firing arrows at the terrifying beast. It was easily driven down the beach, and they followed as fast as they could and continued to chase it away.

"It is scared of us," yelled Maabea triumphantly, as he continued to lead the pursuit down the beach. For a long time they chased the demon beast that held the humans with the white heads within it. It seemed afraid of the arrows and each time it stopped in the air they were able to catch up, always firing more arrows in its direction. This process continued for some time until suddenly it rose high into the air, disappearing over the treetops and into the interior of the island.

Satisfied that it had gone they began walking back to the village only to see it hovering once more over the reef as they neared home. This frightened them and they began to run toward the village, fearing for their families. Before they could reach the chadda's, it rose once more high into the air. All, still fearful, watched it move the opposite direction around the coast and then out to sea, disappearing in the direction of Aahey-kwhade winds.

Breathless, they reached those who now stood near the village on the sand over where the kwentale had been buried. One battered and rotting body lay exposed to the sun.

"What happened?" asked Maabea. "Who uncovered the dead?"

"The demon did," said Tila. "It took one away. It came from the forest and descended to the sand and the sand moved as with the wind in a storm, lifting skyward and exposing the bodies." They had seen the effect of the demon upon the water but those that witnessed what occurred with the sand, were amazed and frightened.

Quickly they covered the remaining body a second time, heaping up even more sand to twice the height as before. The camp was now shifted further down to the other end of the bay. When the corpses had rotted, the bones were dug up and thrown into the sea at the edge of the reef. Tossed far out into the depths to ensure the spirits of the sea kept them.

Although in the time since that last event, no one had come near the shore of their home, there were still kwentale fishing at the edge of the reef and occasionally in the lagoon. Whenever the Jangwa appeared in number they always withdrew and occasionally left when a bigger dange' appeared from time to time. But they always returned and those on Chiö-tá-kwö-kwé did not know how to prevent this from happening.

Their world had changed during the lifetime of those still living, as it had with many generations before them. It seemed things of the spirit world beyond kept appearing, washed up or drifting past and always the odd kwentale, fishing on the edge of their reef. Once a group came and were seen briefly walking on the waves but this perplexed them further. One does simply not walk on water!

And still the ground shook occasionally. At one time small shakes occurred several times in one day. This was far too frequent to be normal and was then followed by a much bigger shake. Once again they delayed the shift to the coast for a few days in case giant waves came for this was before the turtle season started.

Many years passed and many dange' came and went near the reef. They never stayed long but they never ceased to come. Then one day a smiling kwentale with features unlike any they had seen approached the edge of the reef in a small bright colored dange'. As they assembled there he paddled past them to the beach within the gap in the reef but stayed far enough back from the sand, yet not out of reach of an arrow; although Maabea stopped anyone from shooting as his one was alone and not like those who stole fish from their ocean.

"But he comes with the Kwentale," Tila insisted.

"But he is different and his craft is unlike any we have seen and so bright like that of the e-dana-we. We will see what comes of it," Maabea overruled.

Indeed this lone individual gradually approached the beach, got off his craft and waded up to his knees holding something aloft as he placed his hands inside and lifted up something they recognized.

"Nariele," Kaanoa cried. "He brings nariele!"

Indeed the visitor held a coconut aloft and tossed it onto the beach along with the Uhu'a that he pulled it out of. As they stood back he waded out to his craft unaware that Maabea had pulled Tila's arms down as he attempted to shoot.

"No, it is a gift and he leaves without us asking."

The stranger paddled out to the waiting boat, hauling his small kayak aboard and they watched as they sailed off.

"I'm surprised they allowed you to live John," Rajaji said, surprised in the young man's luck. "You know what happened in 2006!"

"Yes, I know. But I feel called to reach them and they were not aggressive in anyway."

"That's not what I saw. When you had your backed turned one pointed an arrow at you but his arm was pushed down by another."

"Really? So one wanted to kill me and one wanted me to live? That is interesting, yet God intervened."

"Maybe," Rajaji agreed.

A year later John was back and once again Rajaji agreed to sneak him out to the island at night where he paddled another kayak to shore, dropping off more gifts of coconut as he had read from TJ Pandit's accounts that they accepted these gifts with much enthusiasm. Once again, he was tolerated and he left unharmed, arriving back for the third time just three mornings afterward where this time he was met by three men and one woman standing on the beach halfway from the water to the tree line. This time he was able to stand on the sand and placed seven *'nareeelle'* as he thought he heard the word he assumed referred to the gifts as they shouted back to those in trees. They spoke rapidly with high-pitched chatter and used quick gestures as he backed away and they moved forward to accept the gifts. One carried a bow and three arrows but back in the tree line John could see many more hiding in the shadows and he became nervous, backing away to his kayak and paddling backwards until far enough away from any potential arrow that might come his way. Again, Rajaji was amazed at his ability to remain unharmed.

"It is the gifts. They love the coconut."

"It is God that protects me," he insisted.

"I think it is the coconuts actually Mr Chau. If you are convinced it is God that saved you from harm you should then try it without the gifts next time, but I do not think you will be so lucky then."

When John returned to Port Blair in 2018 he made plans to sail out to the island again but Rajaji refused to take him. It took two weeks to find someone else prepared to make the trip in secret and it only cost 25,000 rupees to convince Deepak to ferry him to the island. Once again travelling at night and for the fourth time being able to elude any coast guard ships patrolling the waterways, they reached the same beach as before. John launched another kayak, this time a yellow one that was similar to the colored belt that wore around their waists. They were short people but well proportioned and deeply dark over their whole bodies, naked except for the yellow patch they wore around their waist, even though it hid nothing of their genitalia.

The color of the kayak raised a stir. For like Geru, Cho'mal was a favorite of those on Chiö-tá-kwö-kwé.

"It is him," Tila recognized as he came to the sand after a call from Ba, his child. "Maybe he brings more nariele?"

"Should I fetch Maabea?" Nilo asked.

"No, I will go to him this time," Tila said as he grabbed his weapons. They stood afar off and watched as the visitor raised up something round and a fish.

"Fish? Is he insulting us? And look, he brings the moon with him."

"How dare he?' Tila said incensed that this visitor could make such a mockery of creation. With Maabea not here, he yelled and trilled and shook his weapons toward the visitor in his little yellow dange'. "Go away or we kill you," he yelled and heard similar words come back.

"He will kill us?" Nilo asked. "Why does he threaten us?"

"Come here and we will stick you like a pig," Tila yelled as he and the others around him laughed loudly at the joke, before yelling insults at him.

Tila and five others began walking toward the sea and the man backed off when he saw them string arrows to their bows chanting "Be-Cha-Bu" as they did so.

They watched as the visitor tuned his watercraft around and paddled off very quickly.

"Shall I shoot?" Nilo asked.

"No Ba will do it," and in obedience the child sent and arrow flying that reached the dange' but did not slow down the rate of flight away from the island.

"Did I hit him?" Ba asked.

"You might have, but not enough to stop him. I do not think he will come back."

When Maabea returned hours later after the hunt, he was surprised to learn to the return and annoyed that they were insulted in such a way and yet he did not wish to harm this man if it was the same one.

"Yes, he was not a real Kwentale, dark but his features are different and his language stranger. If he returns I will kill him," Tila said.

"Do as you wish," Maabea agreed.

That did not go so well," Deepak observed as John pulled the kayak back into the boat.

"They were angry for some reason. What have I done? Two years ago they seemed tolerant of me, now they are aggressive."

"What did you do different last time?"

"Nothing," John said. "I took gifts then too and they accepted those. They seem to like coconuts."

"Yes, they do like them. Mt TJ Pandit achieved first contact, close intermingling with them on the beach by giving them coconuts, which do not grow on the island we believe. Maybe they were disappointed you did not have any. Maybe they see those as peace offerings and what you had today meant nothing to them?"

"But God is on my side, I told…" and then he stopped. The words of Rajaji from two years prior came flooding back that maybe God was not the reason he was protected in the years before, but the coconut that presented the offering they were

113

looking for. This meeting had certainly not gone they was he expected. Yet the arrow had missed him and entered the waterproof bible that lay at his feet in the open kayak. The bible had not protected him for the arrow had missed, just! But he was confused at the sign and all day while on the ship that sailed away from the island to avoid detection, he mulled over the disastrous and aggressive contact. After long deliberations, he wrote in his journal and penned a letter to his family, resting until his next attempt in the early morning hours of the next day. "Why does this beautiful place have to have so much death here?" he wrote. "I hope this isn't one of my last notes but if it is 'to God be the Glory", he wrote sadly before falling asleep.

He was woken by Deepak as first light approached but it took him three hours before he made up his mind and had the boat come close to the shore, lowering himself into the kayak with more gifts, sadly no coconuts, for there were non on board and he rued not recognizing of what Rajaji had told him. Scared, he began paddling toward the island aware that he may be in danger but unable to pull away from the compulsion to try again for he was determined to deliver news of his God to them.

In the trees, they watched keenly as the visitor once again paddled toward the beach. As he drew nearer, they amassed on the sand and shouted at him to leave, insulting him in their own way. Still he paddled and as he reached the sand and stepped ashore, an arrow pierced his upper chest. The shock sent a cold fear through him as he continued to move forward until another arrow entered his abdomen. Aware his time had come on this earth he reached his hands forward, one clutching his Bible and called out the name of Jesus as more arrows pierced his body. Finally he fell to his knees, breathing heavily only to receive three more before he slumped forward and sank into the sand with his head, pushing the arrows further into his body as his face looked sideways toward some of his attackers. He felt no fear now, but regret engulfed him that he was unable to communicate. Rolling him over they pulled their arrows out and tied a cord around his neck to drag him away. He died looking up at the sky as they pulled him along the beach. Other than killing him via arrows, they did nothing else to the body and left it there for the night.

Seeing the tragedy unfolding before him and knowing what they were doing was illegal, Deepak panicked and took the boat far out into the ocean for the day only returning the next morning to see the body still lying there. Presently members of the tribe appeared. They dragged his body further down the beach where they dug a hole and pushed him into it before covering it over with sand again.

As with others from years prior, Maabea left the body to rot for several months under the sand before digging up the bones, as they had done many years before with the two Kwentale who drifted ashore in their dange'. Taking the bones out to the edge off the reef at low tide, they tossed them into the depths of the ocean. In this way, the spirit of the stranger would not be able to return and harass them.

On Chiö-tá-kwö-kwé, time was seen differently than they way those outside their time and space saw it. If they could visit, even for a moment, the likes of New York, they would be as astounded as we would be seeing an alien world in a distant galaxy. They were isolated in a time bubble, seeing one day as any other apart from stories told from the past as if they had just happened. Unless you talked of now, there was no reference for any previous event.

Indeed the Jangwa, like others in these islands, had not developed a consciousness based on self in any level, and time as we know it, is not something they understand at all well. The great floods, the creation of a man and his creation of a woman from white clay were the only real 'beginnings' they could recount.

In fact, other than the beginnings from the spirits, the great flood and their origins based around their myths, present was based on ritual, rites and change of seasons. No concept of numbers of those seasons or cycles as we have grouped them into years as we record them, actually exist on Chiö-tá-kwö-kwé. Dreams were the only things that changed patterns. To the Jangwa, dreaming held great importance. These controlled the subsequent actions that they take in life. However, in recent times, the dreams became like nightmares and fear gripped the Jangwa.

Tila stood at the edge of the reef, beyond which the ocean plunged to an unimaginable depth. To the casual observer from the modern world, a lone and naked native would be an unusual sight with an ancient design of bow in hand and fish in a woven basket beside him.

But to Tila - this was his world. This was all that existed, and beyond the horizon lay nothing but fear and certain death as far as he was concerned.

Yet he had no idea of the terrible events yet to happen, not too far into the future. What his children would witness would have broken his heart and filled him with dread.

End Notes:

The Sentinelese live lives free of the many cares of the modern world. To them life goes on in cycles, and one day is just like another, and based around the movement of the seasons.

Yet, as you have read this book, they all go about their lives in the same way these occupants of Chiö-tá-kwö-kwé have done for many thousands of years. They deserve the chance to exist undisturbed.

This photo is one taken in 1974. This is where the gift pig was speared on the beach. What you are seeing in this photo is a piece of recorded history that few have ever seen.

Apologies to any who claim copyright on these photos. Most are so obscure, and were so hard to find there was no way to know who the owners are. Accept this as recognition of your photo for the purposes of revealing these beautiful and unique people to the world, so we can understand them a little better and make sure they are 100% protected forever, from the dangers of the modern world.

Glossary:

- 'A'ku gaibí' -   'Don't shoot us!' in Jangil language
- Aahey-kwhade   Wind from the East
- Aalaav   Fire pit
- Aholee-kwhade   Wind from the West
- Aka-Bea   Natives from the north end of South Andaman Island
- Ani-Onu   White Spirits of the sea
- Apilai'oh   A small island at the north of Chiö-á-kwö-kwé
- 'Be-Cha-bu'   'You will die!'
- Belcom   Large leaves of a certain tree
- Chadda   Grouping of communal huts
- Che   Iron
- Chekwe   Type of sea shell
- chik bag chew   Leaf of a tree that menstruating women
- Chiö-á-kwö-kwé Island   Name the Jangwa* call North Sentinel
- Cho'mal   Yellow
- dange'   Dugout canoe
- e-dana-we   Plant with bright colored flower
- eeng   Water
- eh-sep   Ship
- ele-ele   Ambergris
- Embelakwe   Water surge after large earthquake
- ena-enga-le-ye   to mate
- Eneyetokabe   Jangil
- En-iregale   What Onge call themselves
- Etobabu   Flee'

119

- Foga　　　　　　　　large wood burrowing beetle
- Geru　　　　　　　　Red color
- Hullu　　　　　　　　Sick with fever
- Ilo-wa　　　　　　　Cutting the throat
- inenele-geru　　　　　Brown skinned settlers from India
- Jangil　　　　　　　　Extinct race from Rutland Island
- Jangwa　　　　　　　Those on Chiö-á-kwö-kwé (real name is unknown)
- Jarawa　　　　　　　From South Andaman (this name is only used by the Aka Bea people.)
- Kalo　　　　　　　　A type of reef fish
- Kangape　　　　　　Plant
- Kue　　　　　　　　Local pig
- Kwentale　　　　　　Brown skinned foreigners
- Le　　　　　　　　　Honey
- le-mal　　　　　　　Bees wax
- lepa　　　　　　　　Manhood ceremony
- Lololoköbey　　　　　Earthquake
- Meh　　　　　　　　Single poled outrigger
- Nariele　　　　　　　Coconut (none grow on Chiö-á-kwö-kwé)
- Ön-a-bo　　　　　　Pork
- Onge　　　　　　　　From Little Andaman Island   (see En-iregale)
- Oon　　　　　　　　Highest point on island
- Opemame　　　　　　Menstrual ceremony
- Rara　　　　　　　　Tall coastal tree
- taboi-da　　　　　　Type of tree with long straight branches
- Sep'　　　　　　　　Ship
- to-mahe-le-gele　　　Small island on the north
- tonjoghe jah　　　　　Plant once chewed has a narcotic effect on bees
- tugi-ga　　　　　　　Slow burning torch   (kept as backups)
- Uhu　　　　　　　　Honey container

- Uiwa — Southern windward side of the island
- Ung — What the Jarawa call themselves
- Wohen — Adze
- Ya-enga-nga — What other tribes call the Jarawa
- Ya-enga-Paluga-wa Jarawa) — Flesh eaters (Jangwa name for the fierce
- Yaketa — Day after tomorrow
- Yohno — All Andamanese call themselves this as a group (European)

All 'Jangwa' language is a fictional derivative of other local languages

If you enjoyed this book, then please do me a favor and place some feedback on the Amazon Kindle store.

OTHER TITLES BY THIS AUTHOR:

A New Dawn – A Post-Apocalyptic novel set in Madison, Wisconsin in the USA, then moves to the South Pacific as people struggle to survive in the aftermath. (2014) - http://ow.ly/LLXhr

A New Death – (The Sequel). Set entirely in the South Pacific, this story takes the first book further, and is set 25 years after the first book ends. (2014) - http://ow.ly/LLXfl

Origin - Starts around the location of the original event in Madison, Wisconsin, USA. The story highlights those caught up in that location and the early chaos. It also touches on the theme of Dakota* (2014) - http://ow.ly/LLXdR

NYC – Post- Apocalyptic novel based around the ultimate chaos in and around New York City. More violent and disturbing than the others (2015) - http://ow.ly/LLXbf

Anglo – A tale of survival set 35 years after the event in the previous books. Society has regressed and the way of life more akin to medieval times. All is simple and carefree until Islamists arrive and the Rangers intervene. (release in 2015)

Called to be King – A biblical novel of King David…between the lines (2014) http://ow.ly/LLXkv

You can contact me via my website
www.dbdaglish.com

Printed in Great Britain
by Amazon